"I think your need to protect me is all mixed up with what you think is an attraction to me."

"What I think is attraction," he repeated. There was a dangerous edge to his voice, as if she'd just pushed a button that shouldn't have been pushed.

The air between them changed.

He changed.

Collena didn't back away. She wasn't afraid of him. But she was afraid of what she'd started. So much for analysing him and blowing off the attraction.

"Let's test your theory," he said. "Let's see if there's any lust buried beneath all that need to protect you."

And with that, he reached for her.

Before Collena could even catch her breath, Dylan lowered his head and took her mouth as if he owned her.

CAST OF CHARACTERS

Collena Drake – Former cop and head of the task force to find a group of illegally adopted babies, including her own. Her search leads her to powerful Texas horseman Dylan Greer, the man raising her toddler son.

Dylan Greer – The Texas billionaire who had no idea that he was participating in anything illegal when he adopted Collena's son. He'll do whatever it takes to keep the little boy he's raised as his own. Even if that includes a marriage of convenience to Collena.

Adam Greer – Collena's sixteen-month-old son was stolen from her at birth.

Ruth Sayers – Dylan's former nanny who now helps take care of Adam. She's possessive of Adam and resents Collena.

Millie Sayers – Ruth's daughter and assistant nanny. Does she want Collena off the ranch so she can have Dylan for herself?

Deputy Sheriff Jonah Burke – There's bad blood between Dylan and him, and Jonah could be letting their past interfere with the investigation that could save Collena, Dylan and Adam.

Rodney Harmon – The convicted felon went to jail because of Collena's testimony. Now he's escaped and is after her.

Curtis Reese – Adam's biological paternal grandfather. He plans to fight both Collena and Dylan for custody of Adam.

Hank Sayers – Dylan's longtime employee who might also be responsible for a string of deaths that have haunted Dylan for years.

The Cowboy's Son

DELORES FOSSEN

MILLS & BOON
Pure reading pleasure

*This edition published in Great Britain January 2009
by Harlequin Mills & Boon Limited,
Eton House, 18-24 Paradise Road, Richmond, Surrey TW9 1SR*

*First published in 2008 by Harlequin Enterprises Limited under the
title The Horseman's Son.*

© Delores Fossen 2008

ISBN: 978 0 263 87260 6

46-0109

*Harlequin Mills & Boon policy is to use papers that are
natural, renewable and recyclable products and made from
wood grown in sustainable forests. The logging and
manufacturing processes conform to the legal environmental
regulations of the country of origin.*

*Printed and bound in Spain
by Litografia Rosés S.A., Barcelona*

ABOUT THE AUTHOR

Imagine a family tree that includes Texas cowboys, Choctaw and Cherokee Indians, a Louisiana pirate and a Scottish rebel who battled side by side with William Wallace. With ancestors like that, it's easy to understand why Texas author and former air force captain Delores Fossen feels as if she were genetically predisposed to writing romances. Along the way to fulfilling her DNA destiny, Delores married an air force top gun who just happens to be of Viking descent. With all those romantic bases covered, she doesn't have to look too far for inspiration.

To my wonderful editor, Allison Lyons.
Thanks for everything.

Chapter One

"Sir, we have an intruder on the grounds," the housekeeper warned Dylan Greer.

Dylan's stomach clenched into a cold, hard knot. He silently cursed, said a brusque goodbye to his business associate in London and dropped the phone back onto its cradle.

An intruder. Well, the person had picked a good day for it.

It was Thanksgiving morning, barely minutes after sunrise, and he'd given most of his household help time off for the holiday. He was understaffed. Plus, there was a snowstorm moving in. With the already slick, icy roads, it'd probably take the sheriff at least twenty minutes to get out to the ranch.

"Where is he?" Dylan asked Vergie, the housekeeper, through the two-way speaker positioned on his desk.

"The north birthing stables."

In other words, too close to the house. That meant Dylan had to take care of this on his own.

"Call the sheriff," Dylan instructed Vergie as he un-locked his center desk drawer and took out the Sig Sauer that he'd hoped he would never have to use. He grabbed his thick shearling coat from the closet and put his gun and his cell phone in the pocket.

"You want me to tell Hank to go out there with you?" Vergie asked.

"No." Hank, the handyman, was seventy-two and had poor eyesight and hearing. Besides, this might be Dylan's chance to have a showdown with the person who'd made his life a living hell.

Dylan worked quickly to get the information he needed. He used his security surveillance laptop to bring up the camera image of the exterior of the birthing stables. It wasn't the most vulnerable spot on his six-hundred-and-thirty acres, but it did have one major security flaw.

Accessibility.

Anyone could have parked on the dirt road a quarter of a mile away from his property, climbed the eight-foot-tall wooden fence and made their way across the pasture to the stables. Not an effortless undertaking in the cold, but it was doable.

And, on his computer screen, he saw the person who'd managed that feat.

There, next to the birthing-stable doors, was a shadowy figure holding a pair of binoculars. The person was dressed all in black. Black pants, bulky black coat and a knit cap. That attire and those binoculars weren't positive signs. Whoever it was hadn't dropped by to wish him a happy Thanksgiving.

Mercy, did he really have a killer on the grounds?

With everything that'd happened, Dylan couldn't take the chance that this was all some innocent intrusion.

"Lock up when I leave," Dylan instructed the house-keeper from the intercom. "And call me immediately if our *guest* moves closer to the house."

He left through the French doors of his office and stepped into the bitter cold. It wasn't officially even winter yet, but the weather obviously didn't know that—it was a good twenty degrees below normal. The wind howled out of the north, slamming right through his jacket, shirt, jeans and boots. A few snowflakes whirled through the air.

The birthing stables were on the opposite side of the house from where he'd exited, so Dylan knew the intruder hadn't seen him with those binoculars. He ran, following a row of Texas sagebrush and mountain laurel, hoping the shrubbery would conceal him for as long as possible. He wanted the element of surprise on his side. Correction. He *needed* that. Because this person might have already committed murder.

With that brutal reminder crawling through his head, Dylan took out his gun so that he'd be ready. He had to protect his son at all costs, and if necessary, that would include an out-and-out fight. He wasn't going to lose someone else he loved to this nameless, faceless SOB.

Though the cold burned his lungs and his boots seemed unsteady on the ice-scabbed pasture grass, he didn't slow down until he reached the stables. Dylan went to the rear of the building so he could approach the intruder from behind, and peered around the corner. The person in black hadn't moved an inch and was about fifty feet away.

He checked his watch. It'd been nearly fifteen minutes

since the housekeeper had called the sheriff, and there was no sign of him. Dylan decided not to wait.

The wind worked in his favor. It was whipping so hard against the stables that it muffled his footsteps, and he halved the distance before he was heard. Dylan already had his gun aimed and ready when the intruder dropped the binoculars and spun around.

It was a woman.

She was pale and trembling, probably from the cold, and she reached inside her jacket, as if it were an automatic response to draw a weapon.

"Don't," Dylan warned. He wanted her alive to answer the questions he'd wanted to ask for twelve years.

She nodded and without hesitation lifted her gloved hands in surrender. "Dylan Greer," she said.

It wasn't exactly a question so Dylan didn't bother to confirm it. "Mind telling me why you're trespassing on my property?"

She didn't answer. She just stood there staring at him.

Dylan didn't want to notice this about her, but she looked exhausted and fragile. He didn't let down his guard, though. There was too much at stake for him to do anything but stay vigilant.

He inched closer, so he could get a better look at her face. Definitely pale.

And definitely attractive.

Something he shouldn't have noticed, but it would have been impossible not to observe that about her. Her eyes were dark chocolate-brown and a real contrast to the strands of wheat-blond hair that had escaped her black stocking cap.

"I don't know you," he said.

"No."

Funny, he thought he would. Well, if she was the person responsible for two deaths. But he was beginning to doubt that she was the monster he originally believed her to be.

She didn't look like a killer.

And he hoped his change in attitude didn't have anything to do with those vulnerable brown eyes.

"Who are you?" he asked.

"Collena Drake." She studied his face as if her name might mean something to him.

It didn't.

But Dylan kept pressing. "What are you doing here?"

She looked away. "I needed…to see you."

That hesitation and gaze dodging made him think she was lying. "The sheriff will be here any minute to arrest you for trespassing."

"Yes. I figured if you spotted me that you'd call the authorities. I don't blame you. If our positions were reversed, I would have done the same thing."

Her rational, almost calm response confused and unnerved him. "Then why come? Why risk certain arrest?"

And he was positive he wasn't going to like this answer. What would make this visit *that* important?

But the answer didn't come after all. He could see that she was breathing hard. Her warm breath mixed with the cold air and surrounded her face in a surreal opal-white fog. Mumbling something that Dylan didn't understand, she reached out with her right hand, grasping at the empty space, until she managed to catch on to the side of the building. The grip didn't help steady her.

She crumpled into a heap on the ground.

Dylan didn't let down his guard, or his gun, but he

rushed to her to make sure she was okay. She'd apparently fainted, and when he touched her face, he discovered that her skin was ice-cold. After cursing, hesitating and then realizing there was nothing else he could do, he scooped her up into his arms and took her into the empty birthing stables.

He deposited her onto the hay-strewn concrete floor and flipped the switch on the wall to turn on the lights and the heater. Still, the place wouldn't be warm for hours, so he grabbed a saddle blanket from the tack shelf and covered her with it.

Dylan checked the time again. The sheriff was obviously running late, and he debated calling an ambulance. Her color wasn't great, but her breathing was steadier now and she had a strong pulse. This didn't appear to be a life-threatening situation.

Since she had no purse, Dylan stooped down beside her and checked her coat pocket for some kind of ID. He found a wallet, a small leather flip case and keys. He looked inside the wallet and located her Texas driver's license.

If the license was real, and it certainly looked as if it was, then her name was indeed Collena Drake. She was twenty-eight, five-feet-nine-inches tall, and she lived in San Antonio, a good two-hour drive away. Also in the wallet were credit cards and about three hundred dollars in cash, but no photos or other personal mementos to indicate exactly who this woman was.

However, the flip case gave him a clue.

It was a private investigator's badge.

That didn't answer any of Dylan's questions, but it did add some new ones to the list of things he wanted to know about this fainting trespasser.

He pulled open her jacket and immediately saw the shoulder holster and gun. Since he didn't want to take the chance of being shot, he extracted the weapon and put it in his own pocket.

"Miss Drake?" Dylan said, tapping her cheek. He took out his phone to call for an ambulance, but he stopped when she began to stir. "Are you all right?"

Her eyelids fluttered open, and she ran her tongue over her wind-chapped bottom lip. "What happened?"

"You passed out," he informed her. "Are you sick?"

She hesitated, as if giving that some thought. "No. I don't think so."

"Are you pregnant?" Not that there were any visible signs of a pregnancy, but then it would be hard to see a baby bump behind that loose sweater.

Something went through those intense dark eyes. Something painful. "No. Not a chance." Collena Drake held on to the blanket but maneuvered herself to a sitting position. In the process, she brushed against a post, specifically a raised nail head that caught onto her stocking cap. "It's been a while since I've eaten. I'm light-headed."

Dylan shook his head. "For a trespasser, you didn't exactly come prepared, now, did you? You nearly froze to death and you're starving. Is this your way of asking for an invitation to Thanksgiving dinner?"

"No," she snapped. She pulled off her stocking cap, and her blond hair spilled onto her shoulders. She untangled the yarn from the nail and slipped the cap back on. "I didn't come here for food."

He hadn't thought for a minute that she had. "Then, maybe it's a good time for you to tell me why you did come?"

"Because you're Dylan Greer." She inched away from him. "I saw you yesterday. You were in town."

That was true. He had gone into town the day before to do some early Christmas shopping. However, during all his errands, Dylan hadn't seen this woman.

That caused his concern level to spike again.

Because Dylan wanted to make sure she understood that he didn't approve of her, her presence or what she'd done, he leaned in closer. Too close. So that they were practically eye-to-eye.

She didn't cower from him. In fact, her chin came up, and instead of fatigue and frustration, he saw some resolve in her expression.

"What's a P.I. from San Antonio doing following me around town?" he demanded.

Her resolve increased even more. "I've been looking for you a long, long time, Dylan Greer."

And it sounded a little like a threat.

"I'm not a hard man to find. I've lived in Greer all my life. The town is named for my great-great grandfather. And I own a fairly well-known horse-breeding business. My name is even on the mailbox at the end of my driveway."

She made a soft sound of frustration. "You weren't easy to find because I didn't know I was looking for you."

He heard the sheriff's siren in the distance. *Finally.* It was about time. In five minutes, maybe less, he could turn all of this over to the authorities. But he couldn't do that until he learned more about his visitor.

Tired of answers that weren't making sense, Dylan decided to cut to the chase. "Did you kill my sister and my fiancée five years ago?"

Her eyes widened. "No. God, no."

Collena Drake sounded adamant enough, but it didn't satisfy Dylan. "Are you telling me that you didn't know about their murders?"

"I knew. I mean, I ran a background check on you. Their deaths popped up on the computer records. But the computer records didn't say anything about murder."

"Trust me," he snarled. "It was murder. Now, I want to know what you had to do with that."

"Nothing. Until three days ago, I'd never even heard of you."

Yet something else that didn't make sense, especially since she'd said she'd been looking for him for a *long, long time.* "So, what changed three days ago?"

"Everything."

The single word that left her mouth was more breath than sound.

Dylan didn't need the winter to chill him, because that comment put some ice in his blood. He stood and stared down at her. Waiting for an explanation. And not at all sure that he really wanted to hear it.

"I'm a cop," Collena Drake said, getting to her feet.

It was another crazy twist in this crazy encounter. "If you thought that would stop me from having you arrested, you thought wrong."

"I have no expectations about how you will or won't react to me." She hugged the blanket tighter to her chest and waited a moment until her teeth stopped chattering. "Last year I took a leave of absence from the San Antonio PD so I could work full-time on the Brighton case."

"Brighton?" he repeated. Dylan shrugged. "Am I supposed to know what that means?"

"You should. I'm talking about the Brighton Birthing

Center investigation. Last year, the police discovered that the center was a front for all sorts of illegal activity." She paused. "Including illegal adoptions."

His heart felt as if someone had clamped a meaty fist around it. Because last year he'd adopted his own precious son, Adam. And he wasn't just a part of Dylan's life, Adam *was* his life.

"I didn't go through Brighton to get my son," he informed her.

"No. But Brighton still supplied the newborn that you adopted through the law firm you used."

"What makes you think that?" Dylan fired back.

Her jaw muscles stirred. "Because for months I've investigated every detail, every file and every person who had any association whatsoever with Brighton. Then, three days ago, all the pieces finally came together, and I was able to figure out what'd happened."

The siren grew closer, and Dylan knew that the sheriff was now on the ranch itself and headed straight for the birthing stable.

"Are you saying you believe that my son was illegally adopted?" Dylan asked.

"Yes," she answered without hesitation.

Oh, the thoughts that went through his mind. Nightmarish thoughts. Had the birth parents changed their minds about the adoption? Did they want Adam back? If they did, it wasn't going to happen. Adam was his son in every way that mattered, and he wasn't going to give him up.

Dylan pushed aside all the emotion he was feeling and focused on one glaring hole in her theory. "If you thought the adoption was illegal, then why did you come? Why aren't the San Antonio police here instead?"

She met his regard head-on. "I came because I have a personal stake in this."

Outside, the siren fell silent. Dylan heard the tires crunch on the frozen ground as the patrol car braked to a sudden stop.

"Is this your case?" he clarified.

Collena Drake shook her head. "It's not just that I'm the investigating officer. I, too, was a victim of the Brighton Birthing Center. After giving birth there, my baby was stolen."

Dylan was about to ask what that could possibly have to do with him, but the doors burst open. It wasn't the sheriff but Deputy Jonah Burke, a hulk of a man who was armed with a semiautomatic. The deputy definitely wasn't the person that Dylan wanted to see and, judging from Jonah's expression, he felt the same about Dylan.

"Everything okay?" the deputy asked, his attention nailed to Collena Drake.

She let the blanket fall to the floor so that she could again lift her hands in a show of surrender. However, she kept her gaze pinned on Dylan.

"Sixteen months ago, I gave birth to a son," she continued. Her voice cracked on the last word and her bottom lip began to tremble.

Dylan wasn't trembling, but he felt some of that raw emotion himself.

"So?" he challenged.

"*So,* you illegally adopted him. I'm Adam's mother."

Chapter Two

Collena held her breath and waited for Dylan Greer's reaction to what she'd just told him.

She'd braced herself for just about anything. Shouts, accusations, violence, perhaps even an arrest. But neither violence, nor an arrest would stop her from making him understand the truth.

Dylan Greer had her son.

Just silently saying the words made Collena's heart ache. Yes, she'd found her baby—*finally*—but the man who'd adopted him was a massive obstacle who stood in the way of her becoming a real mother to her child.

Collena was prepared to make any and all compromises to be a mother. What she wouldn't do was walk away and not be part of her son's life. No way. She wouldn't do to her child what her own mother had done to her.

"Well?" the deputy prompted. "Is someone gonna tell me what in the sam hill is going on here?"

With their eyes locked, Collena waited to see what Dylan would say. He didn't make it easy on her—she had to wait several long moments.

"I'm not sure," Dylan answered. "But I'll find out."

The deputy turned up the collar on his thick wool coat. "Mind if we 'find out' someplace warmer? I'm freezing my butt off out here. And if this is some kind of lovers' quarrel—"

"It's not," Collena and Dylan said in unison.

But she did agree with the deputy on one thing. She was freezing, too. And she was dizzy. How could she have been so stupid not to eat before she set out to try to get a glimpse of her child? It was an understatement to say she'd been preoccupied with seeing her son, but fainting and feeling weak weren't good bargaining tools for what would no doubt be a major battle with Dylan Greer.

"How about we take this to the house?" the deputy suggested. "I can have a cup of Ina's coffee and you two can decide when you're going to let me know what's going on." He aimed his index finger at Dylan. "But I warn you, if you brought me all the way out here on Thanksgiving for nothing, then even Ina's coffee won't improve my mood."

The ruddy-faced deputy added a lopsided smile to indicate he was only partly joking. Dylan didn't return the smile. The tension between them was almost as thick as it was between Dylan and Collena.

Almost.

"Can you walk on your own?" Dylan asked her. He waited just long enough for her nod before he headed out of the stables and in the direction of his house.

Where her son was.

That sent Collena's heart racing, and it was for all the right reasons. She might get to see her child.

Ahead of her, Dylan took out his phone and Collena heard him make a call. He told whomever answered to unlock his office door and to make sure Adam stayed out of there for a while.

Collena wouldn't be able to see him. Part of her understood that. Dylan Greer didn't know her at all. Judging from the questions he'd barked at her, he thought she might be a killer.

Now, that brought on more than just raw nerves. What had happened to this man to make him think a trespasser was out to murder him? And were his suspicions valid? Collena certainly intended to look into the matter, because if it was true, her son might also be in danger.

"Some advice?" the deputy drawled. "It's not a good idea to trespass on Dylan's property. Since he adopted that little boy, he doesn't pull any punches about stuff like that. He'll have your butt arrested in a New York minute."

Collena ignored the warning and brushed some snowflakes off her face. "Is he a good father?"

The deputy glanced at her as if she were mentally a little off. "Yeah. He is. A surprise, if you ask me. When the two of us were growing up, I never took Dylan for the fatherly type."

Well, the deputy was apparently the only person surprised with Dylan's fatherly attributes. In the past three days, Collena's team of investigators had dug up everything they could on the man, and from all accounts Dylan wasn't just a good father, he was an outstanding one. In addition, he had a sterling reputation and was considered to be an honest, dependable man if not a little ruthless when it came to running his business.

And it was all those things combined that had made Collena come up with her plan.

A plan that had to work. Even though she had no idea

how she was going to convince Dylan Greer to do what she needed him to do.

She studied the man ahead of her. He had the looks to go along with that sterling reputation. He was, for lack of a better word, *golden*. Bronze-colored hair that fell low on the back of his neck. Naturally tan skin. And those sizzling green eyes. Amazing eyes to compliment his amazingly rugged face.

Collena hated that she noticed the last part, but it would have been impossible to ignore. If the world ever needed a cowboy cover model, Dylan Greer would be the perfect man for the job.

She'd expected to feel insecure and inferior around him, what with his money, education and power. There would always be some of that. But Collena hadn't expected to feel the slight tingle inside that reminded her she was a woman.

A hungry woman.

The tingle couldn't have anything to do with Dylan. Low blood-sugar levels were to blame. And Collena refused to believe otherwise. She had a job to do here, and she couldn't let tingling feelings get in the way.

"I take it there's a history between Dylan and you?" The deputy didn't wait for her to answer. "Were you two lovers and then you gave up your baby for adoption?"

"Nothing like that," she muttered. So she wouldn't have to continue this interrogation, she hurried to catch up with Dylan. "Did you hear what I said about being Adam's mother?"

It was a rhetorical question, a way to get the conversation started. Because Collena was dead certain he had heard every single word she'd said back there in the stables.

He spared her a glance and kept walking through the

pasture. "There was no reason to respond because I don't believe you."

Ah, skepticism. She'd expected that, too. "It's the truth. I have proof."

Another glance. This one had some fire and ice to it. He had the eyes for such a range of emotion. Those shades of green seemed both hot and cold at the same time. Right now, they were leaning toward the chilly side, and that chill was all aimed at her.

"I'll be interested in this so-called proof," he said, opening the door. He went in ahead of her and checked out the place before he motioned for her to enter.

Collena stepped inside the toasty warm room, and she could almost feel her body sigh with relief. The deputy came in, shut the door behind him and brushed the snowflakes off his clothes.

Collena soon detected the source of the welcoming heat. There was a massive stone fireplace with flames flickering inside. The place smelled of mesquite wood and the scents from the winter pasture that they'd brought in with them. There was also the aroma of roasting turkey and pumpkin pie. Someone was apparently getting ready for Thanksgiving.

Her stomach growled, but Collena ignored it. She had a more important task at hand.

Dylan Greer's office was exactly what she'd expected. Palatial and functional. Horse-themed artwork on the walls. Rich, glossy woods for the floor and desk, and on the desk was a sliver-thin computer monitor and a gleaming silver tray with coffee, raisin wheat toast, biscuits and crystal dishes of various jams and marmalades.

A photograph next to the computer monitor caught Collena's eye. It was a picture of Dylan holding a baby.

Her baby.

But before she could get a better look, Dylan grabbed the photo and slammed it facedown on his desk. He picked up his phone, punched in some numbers and requested a background check on her.

Which she'd expected. She'd certainly done a thorough check on Dylan.

"Jonah, you can go get your coffee now," Dylan *advised*.

The deputy scowled at what was obviously an order, but he headed for the set of interior doors. However, the doors opened before he could get to them.

A woman was in the doorway. Ina, maybe? She was in her late fifties, Collena guessed, and her copper-red hair was cut very short, less than an inch long around her entire head.

"Where's Adam?" Dylan immediately asked.

"Still asleep. I was about to wake him for breakfast and then give him a bath." She glared at Collena with piercing stone-gray eyes. "Are you the intruder?"

"Yes." The woman's scrutiny suddenly made Collena feel a tad guilty. "I'm sorry that I caused such a fuss."

The woman made a grunting sound of disapproval.

"Go back to the nursery," Dylan told his employee. It was another order. "And stay there until you hear from me."

The woman's sound of disapproval became one of concern. "What's going on, Dylan?"

"I'll fill you in later." He didn't say another word until both the woman and the deputy were out of the room and the doors were closed.

"Was that the nanny?" Collena asked.

He paused so long that she didn't think he would answer. "Yes. Her name is Ruth. If you did a background
check on me, then you also know she was my own nanny
and someone I trust."

"Ruth Sayers," Collena supplied. "Her name did come
up." And she was clean. No criminal record. In fact, not
even a traffic violation.

"Just what kind of proof do you think you have about
the adoption being illegal?" Dylan asked.

"More than enough." Because she was feeling light-
headed again, Collena sank down into the plush saddle-
brown leather chair across from his desk and tugged off her
gloves. "As I said I've been investigating the Brighton case
since August of last year. When I realized just how many
babies had been illegally adopted, I asked for help from the
pediatric community. I was able to get names of adopted
babies, and I compared them to those who had been legally
adopted."

He pushed the silver tray toward her and motioned for
her to eat. When he motioned a second time, Collena
pinched off a piece of raisin wheat toast and popped it into
her mouth. Even though it was cold, it tasted heavenly.

"And you're saying that Adam's name came up on that
list of adopted babies?" he asked. But he didn't just ask. It
was buried under a mountain of skepticism.

She nodded. "Adam's name and one hundred and twelve
other infant boys. There were a lot of them, and that's why
it's taken me so long to find my son."

His jaw turned to iron. He paced a few steps in front of
the fireplace, turned and stared at her before taking one of
the biscuits, opening it and handing both it and the silver
jam spoon to her.

With the hopes that her faintness would go away, Collena smeared some strawberry jam on one half and started to eat. Dylan didn't say anything until she had finished.

"Adam's my son," he insisted. "And I don't really care what kind of proof you have. You gave him up—"

"I didn't give him up."

Oh, that had not been easy to say. Collena had to choke back all the pain and emotion just so she could speak.

"Sixteen months ago, I went into premature labor while I was at Brighton," she explained. "Without my consent, a doctor gave me a strong narcotic so that he could steal my baby. I fought him and his accomplice as much as I could. I managed to escape…eventually. What I wasn't able to do was find my child. Until now."

He cursed. And then as if he'd declared war on it, he peeled off his jacket and tossed it into the closet. He didn't stop there. Dylan came across the room, bracketed his hands on his desk and leaned in so he could stare at her some more.

"And why should I believe you?" he challenged.

Collena tried to keep her voice level. "In my car I have the police and doctors' reports detailing what happened to me and the subsequent arrest of the director at Brighton. I also have the original files. Both sets, the legal ones that Brighton put together, and the illegal ones they figured no one but them would ever see."

He shook his head. "Reports and files don't prove anything about Adam. So what if you had a child? It could have been *any* child."

"Adam's date of birth matches the day I delivered," she pointed out.

"That could be a coincidence. You could be confused about the date."

She took a deep breath and tried to tamp down her frustration. She couldn't say she hadn't expected this though. In fact, Collena figured there'd be many rounds of stonewalling before he started to come to terms with this.

"I'm not confused. There were only four baby boys born that particular day at Brighton," Collena said. "And three are already accounted for."

He waited a moment, and she could almost see the thought process going on behind those eyes. "This doesn't make any sense. I want to talk to Adam's birth father."

"He's dead." And for the time being, that's all she intended to say about her late fiancé, Sean Reese. Thankfully, Adam would never have to have Sean in his life, but that didn't mean Sean's DNA couldn't come back to haunt them. Later, she'd have to explain all of that to Dylan. "Look, I know this is hard to accept—"

"You have no idea."

"But I do. Remember, someone stole my baby and tried to kill me. I have an inkling of what it's like to lose something as important as a child."

Oh, mercy. She felt the tears threaten, and she tried to blink them back. One escaped anyway, but she quickly wiped it away so there'd be no proof of the pain that had ripped her heart apart.

"Look at me," Collena requested. "Don't you see some kind of resemblance between Adam and me?"

It was a gamble, because Collena had no idea if her son did indeed resemble her.

But the gamble paid off.

Dylan combed his gaze over her. Studying her, hard.

And at the end of several snail-crawling moments, he groaned and scrubbed his hand over his face. He dropped down in the chair across from her and raised his head.

"Adam has blond hair and brown eyes," he admitted. "Like you."

The relief washed over her. Not because she doubted this child was hers. No. She was positive of it. But the resemblance might go a long way to convincing Dylan of what she already knew.

It might also convince him to accept the deal she was about to offer.

"I won't believe any of this until I see DNA results," he added a moment later.

Collena had anticipated that, as well. "I already have DNA results to prove he's mine."

"You couldn't."

"But I do. You probably remember telling your adoption attorney that you wanted your baby's umbilical cord to be stored in case it was needed in the future. Since the storage facility was also owned by Brighton, the police got a search warrant to have all the umbilical cords tested. The newborns' identities were all in code, so I knew that one of the babies was mine, it just took a lot of DNA tests to figure out which one."

He pulled in his breath. "And how do you know that you unraveled the code correctly?"

"Because all the other babies have been accounted for. All except Adam. He's the last one on the list."

Collena took the small DNA test kit from her pocket, opened it and wiped the sterile swab on the inside of her cheek. She put it in the plastic bag, resealed it and handed it to him.

"You can send it to any lab you choose," Collena instructed. "Ask for a maternity study. Have them expedite it. Within forty-eight hours you should have the proof you need."

"Need for what?" He stood and dropped the kit onto his desk. He pressed his thumb to his chest. "I love him. Adam is my son."

Collena stood also, so she could make eye contact. "I love him, too. And he's my son."

He cursed, and it wasn't mild. "I can't give him up."

"Neither can I."

"I'll fight this in court." His stare turned to a glare. "I'll have to."

"Maybe not."

Dylan blinked, and his forehead bunched up. "What the hell is that supposed to mean?"

"I know you're a good father." She motioned around the room. "And I can't give Adam all the material things you've given him. Or the stability. Or the respectability."

There was more.

She'd save that for later.

On top of everything else he'd learned, it might be too much for Dylan Greer to hear that they might both lose the precious child they loved.

"And I can't overlook the fact that you're the only parent that Adam knows," Collena added, hoping that she was making her case. "To take him from you now would be as criminal as what happened to me at Brighton sixteen months ago."

His glare softened. "Are you saying you won't fight me for custody?"

"Not exactly."

The softening vanished. "Then, what are you saying?" he asked.

Mercy, she only hoped this sounded better aloud than it did in her head. But it didn't matter if it sounded insane. She had no choice.

"What I'm offering is more of a compromise," Collena explained. "When you weigh all the options, when you think about how we can both have Adam in our lives, there's only one thing you can do."

His glare returned and intensified. "And what's that one thing that I can do?"

Collena braced herself for his reaction. "You can marry me."

Chapter Three

Dylan hadn't thought there could be any more surprises today, but he was obviously wrong. Collena Drake had just delivered the ultimate surprise.

"Marry you?" he questioned.

She nodded and moistened her lips. "I'm Adam's mother. You've raised him, true, but we both love him. It seems...reasonable that we can both be his parents."

"You don't even know him," Dylan tossed right back at her.

"He's my child. *I love him.*"

He couldn't dispute that. He'd loved Adam, too, from the moment that he learned Adam was his. Dylan hadn't had to see him to know just how deep that love was. Still, that didn't mean this woman had a claim to Adam.

"Neither of us wants to lose him," Collena added as if that would change his mind. It wouldn't.

"And you think the solution is for us to get married, even though we're perfect strangers?"

She nodded.

He didn't agree with her. It was an insane proposition. He couldn't do it. Could he?

Oh, man. He hated to even consider it, but Dylan went through a mental list of reasons why he shouldn't. He had no idea who this woman really was. And even if she proved everything she'd said, it would still mean a marriage to a stranger so that he could keep his child.

Dylan wasn't sure he could go that far, nor was he sure he had to. There was rarely just one solution to a problem, even when that problem was as massive as this one appeared to be.

"And what if I say no to your marriage proposal?" Dylan asked.

She took a deep breath. "Then I'll petition the courts to return Adam to me. In my car, I have all the documentation to prove that he's mine and that the adoption was illegal. I've already retained an attorney. He could file my petition as early as tomorrow morning. In nearly all the Brighton cases, the illegally adopted children have been returned to the birth parents. And in those cases where they weren't, it's because both birth parents were dead."

Dylan felt the knot in his stomach tighten. Collena had obviously given this plenty of thought, but then, according to what she had said earlier, she'd had three days to absorb it. He was still trying to come to terms with it, and for him, it was a nightmare.

The adoption attorney he'd used had sworn to him that there were no birth parents in the picture, that they were both deceased. Well, it seemed that either the adoption attorney had been wrong or he was a criminal.

Or maybe this was simply a case of someone on the Brighton staff lying to his attorney.

"In other words, if I don't jump at the chance to marry you, you'll try to cut me out of Adam's life," Dylan mumbled. "This is blackmail, pure and simple. If it's money, you're after—"

"I'm not after your money. In fact, I'll sign a prenup agreement and won't use any of your income or resources for my own expenses. What I'm after is far more important than money. I want a decent life for my child. A life that includes me. You were born and raised here. You don't know what it's like to be considered trash."

That set off some alarms. Dylan stared at her. "And you do?"

"I do." She glanced away for a moment. "I had the misfortune of not being born in the right family. My son has the chance I didn't, and I don't want that chance taken away from him."

Neither did he. Nor did he want to consider what his own life would be like without Adam. Some way, somehow, he would keep him.

"I trust that you don't need an answer right now," Dylan said.

"Of course not." She stood as if prepared to go.

Dylan heard the slight static sound then, and he groaned. Someone was listening on the intercom. He'd forgotten to turn it off earlier when he'd rushed out to find the intruder.

"This is private conversation," he called out. He pointed to the intercom speaker so that his guest would know why he'd said that. No one confessed to the eavesdropping, but Dylan added, "Ask Jonah to come to my office. He'll need to escort Ms. Drake to her car."

Dylan turned back to face her. "I need some time to think this through."

She nodded. "What you mean, is you need to consult your attorney."

"That, too."

"Go ahead. Talk to your attorney. I'm sure he or she will tell you what I've already told you—that I have a legal right to claim the child that was stolen from me." She glanced at the picture that he'd turned facedown on his desk. "May I see Adam?"

Dylan didn't even have to think about it. "No." He wasn't ready to share Adam with this woman.

Heck, he might never be ready to do that.

She stared at him, as if she might challenge his decision, but she didn't. "When we were by the stables, you said something about a killer. Is there some kind of threat to Adam?"

Oh, hell.

Dylan didn't want to go there, because this was exactly the kind of fodder she could use if she challenged him for custody. "I'm a cautious man," he said. "Adam is safe."

"But you said your fiancée and sister were murdered," she reminded him.

"I believe they were. But they have nothing to do with Adam."

"You're certain?"

"Absolutely," he lied.

But the only thing that was absolute was that the two people he loved the most—his sister and fiancée—had been murdered.

Another girl, his high school girlfriend, had been viciously assaulted after Dylan had taken her to the prom. The incident had so traumatized her that she'd moved away from Greer. Dylan, too, had moved away for a while. To San Antonio, right after he graduated from college.

For all the good it'd done.

A woman he'd dated there had also been assaulted one night when putting her recycling bin on the curb. The police hadn't been able to find the person responsible. Ditto for his prom date—no suspects and no arrests. And the local sheriff had ruled his sister's and fiancée's deaths accidental.

But Dylan knew better.

Those two car crashes had not been accidents. And neither had the other assaults. They were connected to him. He was the only common denominator.

Since he was aware of that, he'd learned to take precautions, and he wouldn't let anything bad happen to Adam—accidental or otherwise. In fact, that's the reason he hadn't been seriously involved with any woman since his fiancée's death five years earlier. For whatever reason, it seemed as if someone didn't want him to be happy in love.

"If there's a threat to Adam," he heard Collena say, "then I need to know about it."

And Dylan decided to turn the tables on her. "You said someone tried to kill you after you gave birth."

She nodded. And swallowed hard.

"Then maybe whoever it was will try to come after you again and finish what he started," he pointed out.

"No. The Brighton criminals were arrested. Some are dead and some are in jail."

Because he thought there might be doubt in the depths of her brown eyes, he pushed harder. "You're absolutely positive that the police rounded up all of them?"

"I'm as certain of it as you are of the fact that your sister and fiancée's killer has nothing to do with Adam."

Touché. Under different circumstances, Dylan might have liked her.

"So, why suggest marriage?" Dylan asked.

"On paper, it's the best solution. Adam will have two parents who love him. He'll want for nothing. No shared custody. No one weekend with you, the other weekend with me. And if we're married, if you legally adopted him, then there'll be no way that anyone can cut either of us out of his life."

That last part sounded reasonable, but the whole picture had flaws the size of Texas. "And what about a loveless marriage? Do you really want that?"

Collena made a soft sound of amusement. "From my experience, love is vastly overrated."

"You're too young to be so skeptical," he commented.

"I'm a lot older than my age might imply." She shifted her position. "Look, I'm not some starry-eyed gold digger, Mr. Greer. I don't want a husband, a lover or someone's shoulder to cry on. I don't even want someone to support me or pretend that I matter to him. I just want the best possible life for my son. A life where no one is pointing fingers at him because he's different."

Dylan didn't let himself react to the emotion. To the truthful tone of that obviously painful confession. "If you wanted that, you should have stayed away from him," he challenged.

"I considered it."

And she was serious, too. Serious enough to bring tears to her eyes. It was the second time today that she'd teared up, but even with that track record, Dylan didn't think she was a woman accustomed to showing her feelings. Those tears looked out of place.

"You considered staying away," he paraphrased. "Yet, you came anyway. Lucky me."

"I tried, but I can't give him up." She moistened her lips, looked away. "I lost him once, and I can't survive if I have to go through that again."

Unfortunately, Dylan knew what she meant, but he pushed aside the camaraderie he felt. It was best to keep his feelings toward Collena Drake as detached as possible.

He checked his watch and realized it'd been a good ten minutes since he'd asked Jonah to return. Dylan hit the intercom button on his desk so he could be heard in the kitchen.

"Jonah?"

"He left," Dylan heard Ina, the cook, say. "He said he had another call."

Well, that was just great. Jonah wasn't finished with *this* call. For all the deputy knew, Collena Drake could have been a killer. At a minimum, she'd trespassed, and Jonah should have waited around long enough to see if he was going to have to arrest her for that. Not that Dylan planned to have her thrown in jail. But Jonah didn't know that.

"I can see myself out," Collena insisted. She was heading for the door before she turned back around to face him.

She probably hadn't realized how close they were when she turned around. Mere inches apart.

Both of them stepped back.

"Please think about what I've said," she added.

"Oh, I will." In fact, he would think of little else.

"I'll get my car and drive back to drop off the papers that prove Adam is my son. Or I can have someone bring them to you if you'd prefer."

Dylan didn't want anyone else involved in this just yet. He went to the closet and grabbed his coat and car keys. He wanted to see what kind of evidence she had so he could start looking for flaws in it. He didn't know what he would do once he'd found them, but he wanted all the information about this situation and the woman who'd proposed marriage and then threatened to take Adam away from him.

"I'd also like my gun back," Collena said.

"It's in my pocket. You'll get it back when you're off my property."

Figuring that he needed to go on the offensive, Dylan picked up his phone and pressed in some numbers. "Sorry to bother you on Thanksgiving," he said to the man who answered. "But it's an emergency. Call me the second you have any information on Collena Drake. And I have a DNA test kit that I need you to pick up ASAP and take to a lab."

"Your lawyer?" Collena asked when he hung up the phone.

"A P.I. I want as much information about you as you think you have about me."

And he would get it.

He needed all the ammunition possible to stop this woman who'd intruded into his life.

They went back outside, and Dylan could have sworn the temperature had dropped even more. The snowflakes had picked up, as well. They weren't steadily falling, yet, but it would happen soon. Despite everything that was going on, he couldn't help but think of how Adam would react to building a snowman.

"You're smiling," Collena mumbled.

He put on the stoniest face he could manage. It was easy to do. He was riled at this woman who'd come in unannounced and threatened to tear his life apart.

Dylan motioned toward his truck and unlocked the doors. "I can walk," Collena assured him.

"I don't doubt that, but this will be warmer."

But not faster. She could actually walk across the pasture quicker than taking the roads around the ranch to get to her car, but Dylan wasn't sure how steady she was on her feet. She'd eaten a few bites in his office, but she was still pale and seemed unsteady.

And it irritated him that he was even remotely concerned about that.

This woman could cost him everything.

He wanted to hate her.

What he didn't want was to believe that she was telling the truth. Because if she was, if someone had truly stolen her baby and left her for dead, then she'd been through hell, something that Dylan totally understood.

"I suppose Adam can walk?" she asked.

He groaned. He didn't want to talk about Adam, not to her, but it'd be petty to withhold such simple information. Still, he considered it before he finally mumbled, "Yes."

"And he can talk?"

He bit back another groan. "He can say a few things."

Collena nodded. "Thank you. I know that wasn't easy." She watched as he drove out of the wrought iron gates that fronted the ranch. "I came today, hoping I'd get a glimpse of him through one of the windows. I really hadn't planned on intruding on your Thanksgiving day."

What could he say to that? That she'd gone about it the wrong way? Well, they both knew there was no right way to do this. If she'd come to his door with this bombshell on any day, holiday or not, he wouldn't have let her in.

He made the turn on the dirt and gravel road that snaked against the fenced portion of his property. The snow had already dusted the surface, making it hard for him to see where the road ended and deep ditches began.

Because the silence was thick and uncomfortable, Dylan decided to push her for more information. "Tell me about the father of your child," he said.

Collena took black leather gloves from her pocket and put them back on. She also took a deep breath. "Sean Reese was a lawyer. We'd been engaged nearly a year when I got pregnant."

A year. That wasn't a casual relationship. "You planned a family?"

She shook her head. "No. I was on the pill, hadn't missed taking any, so the pregnancy wasn't planned. When I came home from work the day after I told him, he was gone. He'd moved out and left me a typed letter saying he didn't want to be a father and that he was breaking up with me." She paused. "That's the kind of man he was."

"And he's really dead?" Dylan managed to ask through his suddenly tight jaw. Because he didn't want a guy like that in Adam's life.

"Yes. About six months after he moved out, one of his drug-dealing clients murdered him when he received a guilty verdict that obviously didn't please him."

Dylan hated to feel relieved, but he was. It was bad enough having one birth parent in the picture. *If* Collena was indeed a real birth parent. It was hard to doubt it though, especially when he looked at her mouth.

That was Adam's mouth.

Heart shaped. And capable of expressing a huge range of emotions.

So, if Collena Drake was truly Adam's birth mother, then the question was—what was he going to do about it?

He didn't get a chance to come up with any possibilities because Collena spoke before he had time to think.

"There's something else you should know about Sean Reese," Collena said. Her voice was practically a whisper now, and she looked down at her gloved hands. "I hadn't planned on telling you this soon, but you'll probably find out when you press your P.I. for a deeper background check on me."

Which he would do, especially after an opening like that. "There really is someone from Brighton after you?" he asked.

"No. Not Brighton. The problem is Sean's father, Curtis Reese. He's been looking for Adam, too."

Well, that sounded ominous, and Dylan didn't like where this conversation was going.

"Curtis Reese is very wealthy," Collena continued. "And Sean was his only child. He loved him, and he was obsessive about it. Once he learned that I was pregnant with Sean's child, he became consumed with his unborn grandchild, as well."

Dylan quickly came to a conclusion, but he hoped he was wrong. "Are you saying that this Curtis Reese will try to get custody of Adam?"

"He'll try," Collena confirmed. "I know you don't want to hear this, but since the adoption was illegal, you don't stand much of a chance of keeping Adam."

His jaw tightened even more. "That's debatable."

"It's true. There are things in my past that Curtis Reese will try to use to challenge my own custody. Nothing criminal," she quickly added.

Dylan would have questioned exactly what those things

were if he hadn't seen the smoke ahead. Collena obviously saw it, too; she pointed in that direction.

"That's where I left my car," she said.

With the snow and the wind, it wasn't a day to burn brush. Besides, he'd given all the hands the day off. Dylan took the last turn, dreading what he would see.

There, off to the side of the narrow dirt road sat a dark blue compact car, engulfed in flames.

Chapter Four

Collena saw the fire and smoke.

She felt the instant slam of adrenaline, and she reached for her gun, which wasn't there. Because Dylan still had it in his pocket.

Dylan reacted, too. He caught on to her shoulder and shoved her down onto the leather seat. Hard. Then, he drew his own weapon, threw his truck into Reverse and sped backward to put some distance between them and her burning vehicle.

It was a good decision. With the flames already eating through the interior, the car could explode.

"Do you see anyone?" she asked, trying to get up. But he merely used his muscled body to keep her in place. Protecting her.

More than likely, it was an automatic response, something he would do for anyone who happened to be in danger. And there was no doubt in Collena's mind that this was a dangerous situation.

Someone had set fire to her car.

And that someone could still be around to do even more damage to them.

"No, I don't," Dylan relayed to her. He pulled his phone and her gun from his pocket and handed both items to her. "Call nine-one-one and ask for the fire department."

Surprised, she blinked. "Not the sheriff?"

"Dispatch would only send Jonah back out."

Collena understood. The bitter and perhaps incompetent deputy obviously had some kind of personal grudge against Dylan. Besides, this was a fire, and the fire department would be able to tell whether it was from natural causes or arson.

She had a bad feeling it was the latter.

Collena made the call, and the emergency dispatcher told her that she would send a fire-response team right away.

And then she lay there on the seat, waiting for Dylan to make a decision about what to do. Unfortunately, he was practically lying on top of her. For reasons Collena didn't want to explore, she didn't want to be this close to Dylan. She could feel parts of his body that she shouldn't be feeling.

"I'm a cop," she reminded him. "Let me up so I can see if I can spot any evidence."

He did, reluctantly. "Stay low," he warned. "If someone's out there, he could be armed."

That didn't do much to steady her breathing or heart rate.

While Dylan kept his gun aimed and ready, Collena did a visual search of the immediate area. There were trees, most of them bare from the winter, but there was also a thick clump of massive live oaks, complete with thick branches and green leaves. They completely obscured the view of the ranch. It was the main reason she'd chosen the spot, so that her car wouldn't be seen when she parked it.

Those trees could now be hiding an arsonist.

But who would do something like this?

One answer immediately came to mind. Curtis Reese, Sean's father. Collena hadn't told him that she'd found Adam, but with Curtis's resources, he could have learned that information. Maybe this was his way of warning her not to try to keep Adam from him.

But that's exactly what she was going to do.

"See anything?" Dylan asked.

"It's what I don't see that bothers me. There are no other tire tracks that lead directly to my vehicle."

"Yeah, I noticed that."

She turned her head, and their gazes met. There was plenty of concern in the depths of his green eyes. "The snow might have covered the tracks," she said.

His attention drifted toward those live oaks. "Or someone could have taken this path. Or that one," he said, shifting his focus to the other side of the road where the bare trees were.

He was right, of course. There was another dirt road less than a quarter of a mile away, and it paralleled this one. Someone could have parked there and walked over. Too bad the snow would almost certainly wipe out any tracks there.

"We need to get out of here," Dylan announced.

Collena glanced at her car and saw why. The flames were even higher now. If the gas tank blew, they were a safe enough distance away, but that didn't mean they wouldn't get pelted with debris.

Dylan began to drive in reverse down the road. He took it slowly to avoid slipping into the ditch. If an arsonist was truly still around, Collena didn't want them to be in the woods on foot.

"Both my sister, Abigail, and fiancée, Julie, died in car accidents where fires were involved," he mumbled.

"You think this is related to their murders?" she asked.

A muscle flickered in his jaw. "No one was ever arrested. In fact, the police ruled them accidents. But in both cases, the cars caught fire and that caused the accidents and their deaths. Neither was able to get out alive."

"But why would whoever killed them want to set fire to my car?"

Collena was certain he would dismiss any connection. Just as he'd dismissed the danger earlier.

However, he didn't dismiss it now.

"Most of the women I've been personally involved with have encountered some kind of violence."

"Excuse me?" And Collena held her breath.

"You heard me," he snapped. His posture and tone became defensive. "That's why I've sworn off having a relationship, and it's the reason I adopted a son and not a daughter."

She shook her head. "But Adam—"

"There hasn't been an incident since I adopted him."

Collena pointed to the fire. "What about my car? You don't think that's an incident?"

"That might not be related to the other fires." And he didn't add anything else, as if waiting for her to confirm or deny it.

Sweet heaven, she couldn't.

Dylan finally made it to the end of the dirt path and turned onto the main road that would take them back to the ranch.

"Now you understand why I can't consider your marriage proposal," he continued. "Though my past is only one of many objections I have."

Collena understood. In fact, his past terrified her. But not as much as the alternative of losing Adam. "We might both lose custody if we don't work together."

"Working together," he repeated. "I'll give you that. But marriage is out."

Not being married to Dylan would put a serious wrinkle in her plans. Besides, this fire might not have anything to do with his past or with Sean's father. "Maybe this was some kind of prank. Kids are out of school for Thanksgiving. Maybe someone was bored and decided to light a match."

Dylan didn't answer right away. "Maybe."

Collena released the breath she'd been holding and hoped they weren't deluding themselves.

Individually, they both had some old baggage, but she hoped that it wouldn't surface. Above all, she had to do whatever was necessary to keep Adam safe. And if that meant taking her son and fleeing, she would.

But she also knew an action like that would heavily impact her little boy. After all, she'd be taking her child from the only parent Adam had ever known.

That was the very thing Collena was trying to avoid.

While they sat in silence, Dylan drove through the gates to the ranch. There was still no sight or sound of the fire truck. Of course, it was winter, and the weather wasn't cooperating. Her car was gone, as was everything inside it— including the copies of the documents to prove she was Adam's mother. The only thing left for the fire department to do was tell them how the fire had started.

And then the sheriff could maybe determine who had started it.

Dylan had been with her the entire time, so she knew he wasn't the culprit. Besides, this wasn't his approach to things. He wouldn't have set fire to a car to destroy documents or to intimidate her.

He was a face-to-face kind of man.

"I have a visitor," Dylan commented.

Collena picked through the other vehicles that were near the house and spotted a black luxury car parked in the circular driveway in front. She didn't recognize the car, but she had no trouble recognizing the tall dark-haired man who was pounding on Dylan's front door.

"Oh, God," Collena mumbled.

"You know him?" Dylan asked, firing an accusatory glance at her.

She nodded. "Yes. That's Curtis Reese, Adam's biological grandfather. He's probably here to try to take him."

WELL, THIS WAS SHAPING UP to be the day from hell.

Dylan braked to a halt directly in front of the house and barreled out of his truck. He was not going to let Curtis Reese anywhere near Adam.

"I'm sorry," he heard Collena say. "I didn't know he'd follow me."

Dylan didn't take the time to respond to that. Besides, what could he say? He certainly wasn't going to give her a pass.

Yesterday, his life was as close to perfect as it could get, and now mere hours later, things were tumbling down around him.

In the distance Dylan heard the fire sirens, but he focused his attention on the man trying to beat down his front door. Dylan kept his gun gripped in his hand, and he started up the porch steps.

His visitor whirled around with his tight fist still high in the air. Dylan didn't raise his gun. He didn't issue any threats. He just stared at the man, daring him to use that fist in any way.

Curtis Reese stared back at him.

When Collena had first told him that this was Adam's biological grandfather, Dylan had expected someone who looked like a grandparent. Curtis Reese didn't. Dylan figured he had to be at least in his early fifties, but he looked much younger. There wasn't a strand of gray in his dark brown hair. The man was at least six-four, and he had a muscular build that his Italian cashmere suit didn't hide. And Curtis Reese had a formidable expression on his wrinkle-free face.

"I'm here to see my grandson," Curtis announced.

"Then you've wasted your time," Dylan shot back.

Curtis looked past him, and his equally formidable granite-gray eyes landed on Collena. "Did you think you could hide my own flesh and blood from me?"

"For a while." Collena took the steps slowly, and Dylan hoped she wasn't having another dizzy spell. "It's Thanksgiving, Curtis. Go home and give me a chance to work things out with Mr. Greer."

"What you really want is time to figure out how to steal him from me."

Collena shook her head and slipped her gun into her coat pocket. "I don't have to steal him. You have no right to Adam."

"And this conversation is over," Dylan intervened.

Curtis's gaze snapped back to Dylan. "It's not over. I know what Collena's trying to do. She'll try to make a pact with you to stop me from getting custody. Well, you should know that Collena Drake isn't fit to be a mother. Her own mother was a drug addict and prostitute—did she tell you that?"

Dylan shrugged. "It didn't come up in conversation. Now, are you leaving voluntarily, or do I need to *help* you to your car?"

"I'm not going until I make you understand what an unsuitable mother she is. It's her fault that she was at Brighton, and it's her fault that Adam was stolen. She took a deep-cover assignment while she was pregnant. Something bad could have happened there. And it did. She endangered herself and therefore her baby. I think I can convince a judge that what she did can be construed as child endangerment."

Dylan tried not to react to that, mainly because coming from Curtis, it could be a lie. But then he glanced at Collena. He didn't think it was his imagination that she was even paler now than when he'd first seen her. Later, after Curtis was off the grounds, they would obviously have to discuss this latest allegation.

"Adam's in danger," Curtis said, his voice strained with emotion. "And it's all Collena's fault." He volleyed glances between them. "Did you know that Rodney Harmon escaped from jail last night?"

Collena actually dropped back a step, and Dylan caught her arm so that she wouldn't fall on the slippery porch. He'd never heard the name Rodney Harmon, but he figured soon he'd know why the man had caused Collena to have that kind of reaction.

"Harmon will come after you again," Curtis warned Collena. "And if you're near Adam, he'll come after him, too. You shouldn't be within a hundred miles of that baby."

Collena glanced at Dylan and stepped out of his grip. "Rodney Harmon is the man I helped arrest and put into prison. He was one of the security guards at Brighton. And among other things, he was responsible for…stopping me from going after the doctor who stole Adam."

He didn't have to guess how the guy had stopped her. Dylan had a strange gut reaction to that realization. He wanted to pound the guy to dust because he'd attacked a vulnerable woman who'd just given birth. And why? All so someone could steal her infant son and sell him.

But Dylan had lived the flip side of Rodney Harmon's diabolical plan. He'd adopted the baby that Rodney had helped steal. Dylan couldn't regret that. Ever. But he could regret the pain Collena had gone through.

But maybe that could be overshadowed by Curtis's other allegation. That Collena was responsible for what had happened.

Had Collena assisted Rodney in some way?

Since there was obviously a lot of new issues to discuss, Dylan chose the one that could cause the most serious and immediate problems. "Why would this Harmon guy come after you?" Dylan asked Collena. "Weren't there dozens of cops who helped put him away? Why single you out?"

Collena looked him straight in the eye when she answered. "He blamed me personally for his arrest because

I was the only one who was able to identify him. And I testified against him during his trial."

Hell.

So, there was a new threat—a serious one. And if Harmon had escaped the night before, he could have been the one to set fire to Collena's car. But that was a stretch, since Harmon would have first had to know where Collena was and then follow her.

Still, it wasn't impossible.

But Harmon was a threat Dylan would have to deal with later. Right now, he had to get Curtis off his porch and far away from Adam.

"Look, I have zero patience for you and this visit, especially today," Dylan told Curtis. "Have your lawyer contact my lawyer, and stay away from anything that's mine. And right now, Adam is mine."

"This isn't over," Curtis insisted, though he did proceed down the steps. "One way or another, I will get my grandson. There's not a judge anywhere in the world that will give Collena custody. Nor you, Dylan Greer."

That did not sound like an idle remark. "Been digging up dirt on me, too?" Dylan calmly asked.

Curtis caught the door handle of his car, but he didn't get in. "You bet I have." The man smiled. "That's some dark cloud you got hanging over you. Two women are dead. Others are psychologically scarred for life. It could happen again. And I'm going to use anything I can to get custody of Adam."

With that threat still lingering in the freezing air, Curtis got in his car and slammed the door. Dylan and Collena watched as he sped away, kicking up a spray of snow, dirt and ice. The back end of the car fishtailed on the slick surface, but Curtis continued to speed out through the gates.

"Why don't you come in?" Dylan invited Collena. He took hold of her arm to make her realize this wasn't an invitation she could turn down. "You have some things to explain."

Chapter Five

Collena had hoped to tell Dylan about her past in her own way and on her own terms. She didn't want to have the conversation on Thanksgiving before he'd had a chance to consider her offer of marriage.

But it was obvious this couldn't wait.

He opened the front door, and they stepped back into the warm house. Dylan immediately locked it. Double locks, then he set the security system before he led her in the direction of his office.

They weren't alone in the house. Ruth, the nanny, and a younger auburn-haired woman peered out at her from what appeared to be the family room. There was no sign of Adam, but since Collena had run a brief background check on the staff, she figured the younger woman was probably Millie, Ruth's daughter who'd been raised at Dylan's estate.

There was a lot of disapproval in the women's expressions.

It matched the disapproval in Dylan's.

Oh, yes. She had some explaining to do. However, before she could even begin, her cell phone rang. After one glance at the caller-ID screen, Collena knew it was a call she had to take.

"I won't be long," she told Dylan, who walked into his office ahead of her.

He gave a look that conveyed she'd better not. He practically ripped off his jacket, shoved it into the closet and dropped down into the chair behind his desk.

Because the two women were still lurking nearby, Collena stepped inside Dylan's office, as well, and closed the door. It was a matter of picking her poison—she'd rather have Dylan overhear this particular conversation than his staff. Besides, she apparently didn't have anything else to hide. Curtis had already spilled the unsavory details of her life to Dylan.

"Collena," the caller greeted. It was Sgt. Katelyn O'Malley from the San Antonio PD.

And Collena was almost certain what this call was about.

"Rodney Harmon escaped from jail last night," Katelyn confirmed. "We're doing everything we can to locate him and put him back behind bars."

So, it was true. Curtis hadn't been lying after all. And this added a new wrinkle. "Yes. I heard about the escape. From Curtis Reese. He came to Dylan Greer's ranch a couple of minutes ago."

She risked looking at Dylan, knowing what she would see. She was right. He was glaring at her. And waiting.

"So, Curtis knows that you found Adam?" Katelyn verified. "What about Dylan—how'd he take the news when you told him who you were?"

"We're still dealing with that. Can I call you back, Katelyn? I'm in the middle of something here."

"I'll bet you are. I'll check for updates on Harmon, and I'll also try to find out if Curtis Reese is planning to hang around the town of Greer for a while. Let me know if you need anything else."

Collena assured her that she would, thanked her old friend and ended the call.

"Talk fast," Dylan insisted. "It won't be long before the fire department arrives."

Yes, judging from the sound of the sirens, they were already by her car. Soon, they'd come to the house to do interviews and a report.

"Everything Curtis Reese said about me is true," Collena confirmed.

Judging from the way Dylan stared at her, he hadn't expected that answer.

"My mother was a drug addict, and before she walked out on me, she occasionally turned tricks to pay for her drug habit." She slipped off her coat and eased it onto the back of the chair. "And, yes, Rodney Harmon will probably try to kill me if the police don't find him before he finds me."

"What about the part about it being your fault that Adam was stolen?" Dylan asked.

Collena decided it was a good time to sit. She took the chair across from him. She also took a deep breath and prayed she could explain this without crying. This was painful enough with adding the humiliation of tears.

"When I was pregnant, I was working Special Investigations for SAPD. We got reports about irregularities at the Brighton Birthing Center, but it was out of our jurisdiction. The local sheriff didn't have the manpower or the experience to handle it so he requested our assistance. Since

I was pregnant, I went in undercover. Not at Brighton. But at a nearby home for unwed mothers where I would have daily access to the birthing center. We'd had reports that Brighton officials were pressuring and even coercing these young women into giving up their babies."

"That still sounds dangerous." His eyebrows lifted.

"It was. It was also stupid."

Dylan shook his head. "Then why'd you do it?"

Ah, he'd cut to the chase. "Because my boss asked me to, and I thought I could handle the situation. I thought I could stop what was happening to those young women at Brighton."

His mouth flattened into a thin line. "You put the job ahead of your pregnancy?"

"Yes," she admitted. It wasn't the first time she'd confessed her guilt.

Collena reminded herself of it every minute of every day.

She let Dylan fill in the blanks. Someone at Brighton had gotten suspicious of her. Maybe someone had recognized her as a cop. A former witness or a person involved in a previous case. Or maybe someone at the home or the center had even had her investigated because they believed she was a prime candidate to put her baby up for adoption. It wouldn't have been that hard to find her real identity if someone was seriously looking. And Rodney Harmon had been the one to try to get her out of the picture. Unfortunately, in doing so, Collena had lost the most precious thing in the world.

Her newborn son.

She and Dylan sat there, staring at each other. She didn't

attempt to read his expression, because she knew what he was thinking.

"You can't possibly be any more disgusted with me than I am with myself," she said. "I made a horrible mistake. And I paid for it. I'm still paying for it."

"And now you want me to pay for it, too?" he snapped.

She didn't have time to answer. Two sounds happened at once. There was a knock at the door, and the fax machine began to spit out a sheet of paper.

The door opened, and Deputy Jonah Burke stepped in. He was sporting a scowl, and there were snowflakes on his Stetson and jacket.

"It's Thanksgiving," the deputy greeted. "And it's snowing like crazy out there. How many more times am I going to have to come out to the ranch today?"

"As many times as it takes," Dylan informed him. He stood and went to the fax machine. "Where's the fire chief?"

"Busy with the investigation. He's shorthanded because of the holiday, so he sent me over here to let you know what's going on."

"And what is going on?" Collena asked when Jonah didn't continue. "What happened to my car?"

Jonah lifted a shoulder and couldn't have possibly looked more disinterested. "Somebody burned it."

Both Collena and Dylan shot him a flat look, but it was Dylan who responded. "Obviously. But since you're a deputy sheriff and supposedly in charge of keeping the citizens of Greer safe, I thought you might have at least a professional obligation to investigate a crime."

His disinterest turned to another scowl. "If there's something to investigate, I'll do my job, but the fire department didn't detect accelerant, and their initial impression is that it might have been an electrical problem."

"The car's engine was turned off," Collena informed him. "Hard to have an electrical fire without the engine running."

Part of her wanted to believe an electrical problem was the cause. But this didn't feel like an accident. Her cop's instincts were telling her this was a crime, and apparently Dylan felt the same.

"So you say the engine was off, but you see, I'm suspect of anything you tell me because I already know you're a trespasser." Jonah turned that scowl on Dylan. "Of course, maybe she had a good reason to trespass."

"You got something to say to me?" Dylan challenged, as he gathered up the pages coming from the fax. He took his attention off Jonah and stared down at the papers.

"I made a call when I left here," Jonah explained. "I found out that Ms. Drake here is investigating illegal adoptions. Since you adopted Adam, it's not much of a stretch to think she's investigating you. What'd you do, Dylan? You cut some corners?"

Collena got to her feet and faced the deputy. "Dylan did nothing wrong. If you check the facts, the real culprit is the clinic where Adam was born."

"I don't need you to defend me," Dylan told her.

For some reason, his cold words sliced right through her. But why wouldn't he say something like that? He despised her, especially after she'd just confessed all to him. She and Dylan weren't comrades. Not even close. And he had every reason to try to remove her from the picture.

Dylan went to his computer and typed something before he continued. Collena got just a glimpse of it. It was an e-mail requesting a background check on Curtis Reese. "Tell the fire chief that I want a report of his preliminary findings," Dylan told Jonah. "And close the door on your way out."

Jonah looked ready to explode over what was obviously another order—a rude one, at that—but he didn't. However, he did mumble something profane before he exited and slammed the door behind him.

Dylan walked closer, until he stood right behind her. What he didn't do was speak. When the silence became uncomfortable, Collena whirled around to face him. Best to go ahead and get this latest argument out of the way.

But she didn't see an argument in his eyes.

She was too close to him.

Something passed between them. A shiver of energy. Something warm.

No, it was *hot.*

Much to her disgust, Dylan could make her feel things she shouldn't feel, and he could accomplish that by merely being close to her.

Collena shook her head to clear it. She refused to let her thoughts and feelings go in this direction. Dylan was merely her son's adopted father. That was it. There could never be anything between them.

Well, nothing except that stir of heat that wouldn't go away.

"The P.I. already sent me a preliminary report on you," Dylan said.

That drew her back to her senses.

Dylan showed her the top sheet of the papers he'd taken from the fax machine. It was indeed a report that included the basics: her name, address, age, height and weight. All bits of info taken from her driver's license, no doubt.

The next page was a copy of a newspaper article where she'd gotten an award for outstanding service for uncovering the criminal activity at the Brighton Birthing Center. There was no picture because Collena hadn't attended the ceremony. Nor had she picked up the award. She'd ripped it to bits after her lieutenant had delivered it to her apartment.

"That award should have been for my stupidity," Collena mumbled.

Dylan didn't respond to that. He simply flipped over to the next page.

There was a picture this time.

It'd been taken as part of the police report after she'd clawed her way out of those woods near Brighton and made it to the local sheriff's office. The photo showed the torn, dirty hospital gown that was practically hanging off her body. Her battered face. Her hair matted with her own blood. A busted bottom lip. And the bruises and scrapes on her hands and knees. She looked a half-step away from death, which wasn't too far from the truth.

She'd come too close to dying in the woods.

The police report indicated how close to death she'd been. It also indicated that she'd recently given birth, and that would hopefully convince Dylan that she wasn't lying about being Adam's mother.

Dylan stared at her. "I don't want to feel sorry for you."

That improved her posture. Collena snapped her shoulders back. "Good. Because I don't want you to feel sorry for me, either. I was a cop. I knew the risk before I ever stepped foot in Brighton."

"You couldn't have anticipated that kind of risk. And you didn't deserve that." He shook his head, and his nostrils flared. "What did Rodney Harmon use to put those bruises on you?"

It took her a moment to answer. No more stiff shoulders. She automatically slumped. "His fists and the gun he took from me when I went into labor. I was trying to fight him off because the doctor had just left the room with Adam."

His jaw muscles moved. "So, Adam wasn't there when you were getting the hell beat out of you?"

"No. Thank God. And the fight didn't last that long. Harmon gave me some kind of heavy narcotic, and after I escaped, I don't remember anything until I woke up in the woods." She paused a moment to gather her composure. "My advice? Shred that picture. Forget that you ever saw it. I don't want it to play a part in your decision as to what we're going to do about Adam."

"My decision," he said. He tossed the papers onto his desk and groaned. "You come here to my home and deliver a bombshell, along with a would-be killer on your trail. And as an added bonus, I've had to deal with Adam's biological grandfather, a man who can challenge us both for custody."

"I'm sorry—"

"Don't," he warned. He stepped farther away from her. "I want to hate you. But I can't. Because I can see the pain in that picture. Hell, I can see the pain in your eyes right now."

"That pain's in your eyes, too."

Dylan immediately looked away. "I won't feel sorry for you and I won't be attracted to you."

Collena blinked, certain she'd misunderstood him. Mercy, had he noticed the way she'd looked at him earlier? With lust in her eyes?

Oh, this was not good.

She actually welcomed the knock on the door. They obviously needed some kind of interruption, because there was nothing that either of them should say about his attraction remark.

"It's me," a woman said from the other side of the door. Collena recognized the voice. It was Ruth Sayers, the nanny.

Dylan reached behind him and turned Collena's photograph facedown. "Come in, Ruth."

The woman opened the door, but she wasn't alone. Her daughter, Millie, was with her, and the pair stood in the doorway.

Collena got a better look at Millie then. She was a younger version of her mom, with fiery red hair and piercing gray eyes. However, Millie had a calmness and serenity about her that Ruth lacked.

"The fire chief said I'm to tell you that he'd be in touch with you," Ruth told Dylan. "Jonah's still here though." She pointed her finger at Collena. "Is he planning to arrest that woman for trespassing?"

Dylan pulled in a weary breath. "This is Collena Drake, and there's a very good possibility that she's Adam's biological mother."

Ruth frantically shook her head, but her daughter, Millie, had a different reaction. She merely stared at Collena. Examining her.

"Does she have any proof of what she's saying?" Ruth snapped.

"Some," Dylan confirmed. "It'll take a couple of days to get the DNA results back. Or I might be able to get the results sooner if I can get the tests from the lab where she had Adam's stem cells tested."

"Adam has her mouth," Millie whispered, nudging her mother with her elbow.

Collena was so relieved she couldn't speak. Another person was confirming that there was a resemblance between her son and her.

"Her eyes, too," Dylan added.

Just that bit of information nearly brought on the tears, but Collena blinked them back. However, it didn't stop her longing to see her child. She'd gotten only the briefest glimpse before the doctor at Brighton had whisked Adam away.

Ruth shook her head. "I don't see any resemblance. Lots of babies have blond hair and brown eyes."

"Someone used the intercom earlier to listen in on the conversation I was having with Collena," she heard Dylan say. He obviously wasn't planning to address Ruth's comments. "Any idea who would do that?"

So much had happened with the fire and Curtis's visit that Collena had practically forgotten about that. But was it even important?

"Are you accusing me of eavesdropping?" Ruth asked. And she looked as if he'd slapped her.

"I'm merely asking a question." Dylan's tone certainly wasn't accusatory, but he did sound adamant about getting to the bottom of the situation.

Unfortunately, the eavesdropping was nothing compared to other things that could be brewing. And Collena thought she knew who was behind them.

Rodney Harmon.

He was the most likely candidate for setting her car on

fire. She couldn't imagine Curtis traipsing around the woods in his pricey suit. Nor could she see either Millie or Ruth doing the same.

Eavesdropping, yes. Arson, no.

But now the question was—how had Rodney found her so quickly? She'd been in Greer for the past eighteen hours, and that would have put her already there in town right about the time that Rodney was escaping.

"I don't know who listened in on the intercom," Ruth finally answered. "Ina, maybe. She probably turned it on when she told you about the intruder and then forgot to turn it off."

It seemed reasonable to Collena, but there was something in Dylan's scrutinizing stare that made her wonder if it sounded reasonable to him.

"I've got things to do," Ruth declared. "If you want to accuse me of anything else, you'll find me in the nursery."

Dylan didn't make any attempt to apologize or follow the woman. Probably because he heard the same sound she did. There were thudding footsteps making their way down the hall, and for a moment, she braced herself for yet another confrontation with Curtis. Or worse. She prayed that Rodney Harmon hadn't wormed his way into the house.

But it wasn't either of them.

It was Deputy Jonah Burke.

"Well, thanks to you, I'm stuck here at the ranch for Thanksgiving," Jonah complained, aiming that complaint at Dylan. "The fire chief just called. The road between town and here is now officially closed."

"Closed?" Collena repeated, groaning. Well, that was just *wonderful*.

She had no car and no way to leave. This day just kept

adding more and more obstacles. She wanted Dylan to get that DNA test to the lab, and that wasn't going to happen with the roads closed.

"Jonah, I'll make up the upstairs guest room for you," Millie volunteered. She stopped though and looked at Dylan. "What about Ms. Drake? Should I get a guest room ready for her, too?"

The impact hit Collena full force. Yes, the road closure would hinder the DNA test and getting replacement copies of her documents, but if Dylan actually let her stay, then she would be under the same roof as Adam.

She might get to see her son.

But she rethought that when she and Dylan turned toward each other at the same moment. That wasn't exactly a welcoming or inviting look he was giving her.

"She'll stay," Dylan said as if he were speaking profanity. He turned to Millie. "Have Hank check the security system. I want all perimeter and internal alarms set to the highest levels. Lock all the doors and windows. Make sure no one gets in without my permission."

Millie's eyes widened, and she nodded. "Dylan, are you expecting trouble?"

"Trouble's already here," he mumbled. "There's a fugitive on the loose," he added in a louder voice, apparently for Millie's ears. "He's dangerous, and I don't want him anywhere near the house."

"What about Adam?" Millie stared at Collena when she asked that question. "What should we do with him to make sure he's…safe?"

Safe, and away from Collena.

"Keep Adam in the nursery until you hear from me," Dylan ordered.

Another nod and Millie walked away, apparently ready to do her duty by making sure Collena didn't see her little boy.

Dylan would have walked away, as well, if Collena hadn't grabbed his arm. "Adam has my eyes. My mouth. My hair. He's my son, and I want to see him."

She could see the debate start. It seemed to make its way through every muscle in his body.

Dylan glanced back at the photo of her that he'd turned facedown on his desk. He was likely feeling sorry for her again. Part of Collena despised that—she hated pity—but another part of her was willing to do anything to see her child.

That included begging.

Still, she wasn't certain that even begging would be enough to convince Dylan.

They stood there. Long, long moments. While his mental debate continued. Collena had her own. To speak or not to speak. And she decided there was nothing she could say that would help her cause.

He groaned softly. "Come with me," he finally said. "And don't make me regret this."

Collena was too afraid to hope that he was leading her in the direction of the nursery.

Chapter Six

Dylan knew this could be a huge mistake.

After the incident with the car fire and Collena's suggestion of marriage, he wanted nothing more than to distance himself from the woman who could take Adam away from him. But he also knew that distancing himself wouldn't make this situation go away.

One way or another, he had to convince Collena that he should be the one to raise Adam. He couldn't do that if they were at each other's throats. And as for marriage for the sake of them sharing custody? Well, that was an absolute last resort, but he wasn't ruling it out just yet.

Dylan led Collena through the maze of corridors in the sprawling house. Nearly ten thousand square feet was more than enough room to bring up an active child. He'd had fatherhood in mind when he made renovations several years earlier.

He stopped for a moment outside the nursery door and looked back at Collena. She was nibbling on her bottom lip and showed more nerves than she had when facing down the car fire and Curtis Reese.

"I'm scared," she admitted.

"Me, too," Dylan acknowledged.

Her mouth quivered as if threatening a smile. Dylan figured it'd been a long time since she'd made that particular facial expression. But the smile didn't materialize. Instead, she squared her shoulders and took a deep breath.

Dylan did the same, and he opened the nursery door.

The room was empty.

Because of the leftover adrenaline, he felt another jolt of concern, but then reminded himself that it wasn't unusual for Ruth and Adam to be away from the nursery. Just because they weren't there in the room didn't mean that someone like Curtis Reese had kidnapped his son. He stepped into the room and pressed the button to turn on the house intercom.

"Ruth?" Dylan called out.

It only took a few seconds for the nanny to answer. "Adam and I are in the playroom."

"This way," Dylan instructed Collena, leading her back through the corridors. He hated that edgy feel of the adrenaline and hated even more that it was now associated with his son's safety. Since he'd had five years with no incidents, he had thought they were safe.

He'd obviously thought wrong.

"Does Adam really look like me?" Collena asked.

He stopped, turned around and considered lying. But he didn't after he combed his gaze over Collena's face. "He's the spitting image of you."

Her bottom lip trembled a little, and she blinked hard. "Thank you." But then she hesitated and stared at him. "You're being nice to me because of that picture. I asked you to forget about it."

Why, he didn't know, but he stepped closer, violating

her personal space. "I'm not being nice to you. If I had my way, you wouldn't be here at the ranch and you definitely wouldn't be on the verge of going into the playroom."

She lifted her shoulder. "So, why am? Why are you letting me see Adam?"

"Because I don't think I have a choice. We're each other's obstacles. You want what I have, and I don't want to give him up. Somehow, we have to work through that, and working through issues is something that I'm usually pretty good at doing."

"I offered a solution," she reminded him.

"I don't call that a solution." In fact, he didn't know what exactly to call her marriage proposal.

Since marriage was the last thing he wanted to discuss, Dylan turned and started walking again toward the playroom. Collena was right behind him. And with each step, he dreaded this meeting even more.

Yet, he knew it was inevitable.

If he didn't allow Collena to see Adam, then tomorrow when the roads were clear, she'd no doubt start legal proceedings to get custody. So, he wasn't being nice. He was doing what he had to do to keep things amicable between Collena and him.

When he reached the set of playroom doors, Dylan didn't pause. He didn't dare. Because he might change his mind. It was like ripping off a bandage. Fast, but definitely not painless.

He threw open the doors.

Dylan spotted Ruth first. She was sitting in a recliner with a paperback clutched in her hand. Adam was on a toy car that he was scooting around the room. He looked up, spotted Dylan and smiled the smile that always made him feel on top of the world.

"Is there a problem?" Ruth asked. Her eyes went straight to Collena, and the nanny got to her feet.

"No problem," Dylan assured her.

Ruth made a nasally sound to indicate she didn't buy that. "Then why is that woman here?"

Good question. But Dylan kept that remark to himself. Instead, he stood back and watched as Collena took short cautious steps toward Adam.

The little boy stopped and eyed the stranger who was approaching him. Adam didn't smile. Nor did he back away as he sometimes did with people he didn't know. He simply studied Collena as she stooped to Adam's eye level.

"Hi," Adam said, using his latest favorite word. Except it sounded more like "i."

"Hi," Collena answered. Her voice was clogged with emotion.

Neither Dylan, nor Ruth said a word, but their gazes met, and he could tell that Ruth saw what Dylan had already known.

This was definitely mother and son.

Collena dropped down onto the floor, sitting directly across from Adam, and the two just watched each other. Adam babbled something, reached out and touched Collena's hair, which was barely a shade darker than Adam's own.

That one touch seemed to open the floodgates for Adam. With help from Collena, he climbed off the toy car, took a picture book that was lying on the floor and toddled back to Collena. Adam thrust the book toward her, and Collena took it and began to read to the child.

The simple gesture got Dylan right in the heart. Adam was more accepting of Collena than he wanted his son to be.

However, he didn't have time to react beyond that because his phone rang. Dylan extracted it from his pocket and checked the screen. It was from Mason Tanner, the P.I. friend who'd sent him those faxes about Collena. Dylan had e-mailed the man shortly thereafter and asked him to do a background check on Curtis Reese.

Because he didn't want Ruth or Collena to overhear this particular conversation, Dylan stepped into the hall to take the call.

"Please tell me you found something on Curtis Reese," Dylan said, commencing with a greeting.

"I did. Thankfully, his life is somewhat of an open book. That's the good news. The bad news is that he's staying at the hotel in Greer and is literally less than eight miles from your doorstep. He's not alone, either. He has his lawyer and a pair of private investigators there with him. And he has power, Dylan. Lots of it. Along with a couple of judges in his pocket."

That was not what Dylan wanted to hear. "Are you saying he could actually win a custody battle?"

"Absolutely. From what I can see from the outside looking in, he can make a case against either you or Collena Drake. Yours is a no-brainer. The adoption was illegal, and that means legally you have no claim to Adam."

Dylan felt as if someone had sucker punched him. "I've raised him since birth."

"That won't negate the fact that the adoption was illegal. I'm not a lawyer, but Collena obviously has the strongest claim for full custody."

He felt another punch. "Once she has proof that she's Adam's mother."

"Oh, there's proof already. I checked the lab where you'd stored Adam's umbilical cord. They're the ones who ran the DNA test for the police, and Collena's DNA is on file because she's a former cop. Adam is Collena's son, all right. No disputing that."

That one was more than a punch. Dylan was grateful for the brief period of silence that followed. He needed it to come to terms with the fact that Collena had been telling him the truth.

Hell.

And the truth was that he could lose Adam.

"Collena has the best claim for custody," Mason Tanner repeated. "Unless, of course, Curtis Reese is able to prove she's unfit in some way."

And Curtis just might be able to do that if he could prove that Collena had endangered her unborn child by going on an undercover assignment. A good lawyer could argue that, and Curtis would almost certainly have a good lawyer. Heck, he'd have an entire team of them.

"What about Curtis Reese himself—what kind of dirt could you find on him?" Dylan asked.

"Nothing, other than rumors that he owns those judges and a few politicians. He was born stinking rich, inherited his family's chain of hardware stores, and then added to his wealth through what appears to be legal means. He's considered a good, upstanding citizen by most. And now that his less-than-stellar son is dead, there isn't even a hint of danger in any facet of his life. He comes off like a Boy Scout, Dylan, and that's not good news for you."

It wasn't. His worst fears had been confirmed—he could lose Adam.

"Keep digging," Dylan ordered. "I want any and every thing that you can find on not just Curtis Reese, but Collena Drake and the man who recently escaped from jail, Rodney Harmon."

"I will, but you have to start looking at the likelihood of a serious custody battle. Or some kind of settlement with Collena. If you can't buy her off, then if I were you, I'd be hoping that she's a reasonable woman."

Dylan clicked the end-call button, slipped the phone back into his pocket and leaned against the wall. His lungs felt heavy, as if he'd taken in too much air, and every muscle in his body was in a knot.

What the hell was he going to do?

He turned and opened the door just slightly so he could see inside the playroom. Ruth was in the chair, and she was glaring at Collena. However, Collena was oblivious, because her attention was focused solely on Adam, who was back on his toy car. His son was grinning from ear to ear and babbling happy sounds.

Collena turned and spotted him in the doorway. She, too, was smiling, and there were tears of joy in her eyes.

Dylan didn't waste any time. There wasn't a reason to delay this.

He knew what he had to do.

He motioned for Collena to come to him. Her smile faded, probably because she anticipated that he'd gotten some bad news from the phone call. She got up from the floor and, without breaking eye contact with him, she made her way to him.

"What's wrong?" she asked.

"Everything." Dylan cleared his throat. He partially closed the door, only leaving it open a small crack. "If your marriage proposal is still good—I'm accepting it."

OF ALL THE THINGS that Collena had expected to hear Dylan say, she hadn't expected that.

"You're accepting my marriage proposal?" she asked, certain she'd misunderstood him.

He nodded. And he looked as if he were facing a firing squad. "The P.I. I just spoke with confirmed that you're Adam's biological mother. He also believes that Curtis Reese has a chance of getting custody of Adam."

"He does," Collena agreed, speaking around the lump in her throat. That's why she'd suggested marriage in the first place. She didn't have the resources and political contacts to fight Curtis, but Dylan did. With Dylan's help, she could get custody of her child.

Her plan was working. That was the good news, but she knew they had a long fight ahead of them. This was just the first step.

"I thought we stood a better chance of winning if we were together," Collena added.

Dylan huffed. "Of course, a judge might see right through our convenient relationship."

"I don't doubt that, either, but Curtis is a widower, and I think a judge would be more likely to keep Adam in the home where he was raised and with parents who've made a commitment to give him the best life possible. We'll just have to be honest and not hide the reason we're getting married. I'm hoping our marriage will prove to the judge that we're willing to do anything for Adam's happiness. Curtis can't compete with that."

His eyes snapped to hers. "You really think we can pull this off?"

"I don't think we have a choice. And believe me, for the past three days, I've studied all the options. If I'd been able to come up with something better, I would have gone in that direction."

"I'll bet you would have," he mumbled. He took a hard breath and opened his mouth to say something. However, Ruth interrupted him.

With Adam in her arms, Ruth threw open the door. "It's time for Adam's bath," she announced.

Collena desperately wanted to spend more time with her son, but she also needed to work out some details with Dylan.

Apparently, they were getting married.

Just thinking that sent a rush of panic through her. She'd come up with the plan before she'd met Dylan. Before she'd realized that she was attracted to him. She wanted her son, but she didn't want a relationship with Dylan. Not with her past. And not with her excess emotional baggage. She still hadn't gotten over the painful relationship with Adam's father.

Falling for him could ruin everything she'd planned.

Collena took both a step back, both emotionally and physically, and let Ruth walk past them. Adam gave them a little wave as Ruth carried him down the hall.

She and Dylan stood there in silence. He was no doubt thinking of the enormous impact of what he'd just done. Collena knew that impact, as well.

"Don't mention the marriage to anyone just yet," Dylan finally said. "I want to be the one to tell the staff."

"Certainly." Though Collena figured that wouldn't be a

pleasant conversation, especially when it came to Ruth. The woman obviously loathed her and was more than just staff. She was family.

Dylan checked his watch. "I need to make some calls, and you probably want to freshen up. I'll show you to the guest room."

Collena nodded and followed him. "When you talk to your lawyer, you'll want to make sure that we can keep the custody hearings here in this county. Curtis has a lot of powerful friends in San Antonio."

"So, I've heard."

No doubt he'd learned that from that phone call. "Before I came here, I sold everything I own. It should be enough to cover legal expenses. What I don't have are Curtis's contacts in the judicial system." She paused. "I'm hoping you do."

"I haven't bribed politicians and judges, if that's what you mean, but people know me in this county. Besides, losing isn't an option."

Collena believed him. She *had* to believe him. She hadn't come all this way to fail.

"You'll join us for Thanksgiving dinner?" Dylan asked, stopping outside one of the doors in the long corridor of rooms.

It took her a moment to shift gears in the conversation. "Yes. Thank you." It would get her more time to spend with her son.

"In the meantime, I'll have Ina bring you a tray so you'll have something to eat."

Collena didn't refuse that, either. She was still feeling a little light-headed, and she didn't want that with all the critical things going on in her life.

Dylan didn't say anything else. He merely opened the door, motioned for her to go inside and walked away. Collena stood there, watching him, and praying that this plan would succeed.

She stepped inside. The light was already on, so she had no trouble seeing the guest room. Or rather, the guest suite. There was a sitting room with a bay window to her right, and the bedroom and bath were to her left. Like the rest of the house, it was tastefully decorated in warm neutral colors with a dark hardwood floor dotted with Turkish rugs.

Collena went inside and sank down onto the taupe-and-cream-colored chair in the sitting room. She felt drained and exhausted, but like Dylan, she had some calls to make. She took out her phone, just as someone knocked. She didn't even have time to get out of the chair before the door opened and Millie walked in.

"Oh, I'm sorry," Millie immediately said. "I thought you were still with Dylan." She lifted her arms to show Collena a stack of clothes. "We're close to the same size, and I figured you could use these, especially since we don't know how long you'll be here with the snow and all."

Collena stood and took the clothes from her. "Thank you."

Millie shrugged. "It's the least I could do, considering your car caught fire."

The words were right. Kind, even. But the kindness didn't make it to Millie's eyes. In fact, Collena got the same cold vibes from Millie that she did from her mother, Ruth.

The woman glanced around before her attention came back to Collena. She hesitated, licking her lips. "Is it true? Are you really Adam's birth mother?"

Collena nodded.

"Oh." And that's all Millie said for several seconds. "But you gave him up for adoption."

"Someone stole him from me," Collena corrected. She left it at that. The sanitized version was best for now. Later, maybe Dylan would explain everything to Millie and the rest.

Another "oh" from Millie. Another hesitation. Millie's breathing was suddenly uneven. "Well, if you need anything else, just ask. The phone there is a private line, in case your cell phone doesn't work out here. Sometimes, service is spotty." She went to the intercom speaker on the table next to the chair and pressed some buttons. "And if you need someone in the house, like the cook, for instance, all you have to do is hold down the talk button. Someone will answer. You don't have to bother Dylan or anything. He has enough to deal with right now."

Now, it was Collena's turn to say, "oh." There was nothing chilly about that remark, but it was, well, territorial.

Did Millie have feelings for Dylan?

If so, this was about to get very messy.

Millie mumbled a goodbye, and as soon as the woman was out the door, Collena closed it and locked it. She didn't want anyone walking in on the phone call she was about to make.

She took her phone from her pocket, flipped it open and pressed in the numbers to her friend and former coworker, Sergeant Katelyn O'Malley.

"Katelyn," Collena said when she answered. "I hate to bother you on Thanksgiving—"

"You're not bothering me. Thanksgiving dinner is still

hours away, and you got me out of cooking duty. I owe you, girl. I'm not into basting turkeys."

"We'll work something out," Collena joked. But the light tone was a facade. She was terrified of what Katelyn might or might not have learned.

"I've been doing some checking on a few of the citizens of Greer," Katelyn continued. "One thing that really stuck out was Deputy Jonah Burke. Have you met him yet?"

Collena didn't like the sound of this. "Oh, yes. Because of the snowstorm, he's stuck in the house with us."

"Well, then, you better hope the roads clear soon. He's had two suspensions from the job and even had criminal charges filed against him for stalking. The charges were dropped when the person who filed them was killed. That person was Dylan Greer's sister, Abigail."

"Dylan's sister?" Collena certainly hadn't expected that. "Why is Jonah still on the force if he was stalking her?"

"Law of supply and demand. Apparently no one else in Greer wants his job. Still, Jonah's not well liked, and even the sheriff doesn't have much good to say about him."

Neither did Collena. "I'll make I sure lock my door tonight."

"Don't lock it just for Jonah Burke's sake. You need to keep an eye out for two of Dylan's employees, Ruth and Millie Sayers. Get this—both have been under psychiatric care since Dylan's sister was killed five years ago."

Another surprise, but it wasn't totally unexpected. "I think they were very close to her. And her death was unexpected. And suspicious."

"That, too. I plan to look a little harder at that, especially if Deputy Burke might have had a reason to kill this woman."

Katelyn was right. The stalking charge would give Jonah motive, and since he was a deputy, he already had the means. That only left the opportunity, and in a small town like Greer, there should have been plenty of opportunities for the deputy to go after the woman. So, had his involvement been covered up?

"There's more," Katelyn continued. "Millie was dating Burke at the time he was supposedly stalking Dylan's sister."

"You're kidding."

"I wish I were. I wish you'd get out of that house ASAP. I don't think it's safe for you there, Collena."

"I can't leave. I want to be here with Adam."

"I know. I know," Katelyn repeated. "Just be careful, okay?"

Collena assured her that she would, ended the call and put her phone on the table.

Mercy, what was going on here?

In addition to the tangled web between Dylan's sister and the surly deputy, there was that whole issue of psychiatric care for Ruth and Millie. Did Dylan know about this? He would almost have to with both women living under his roof. Unless they'd intentionally kept it from him.

Those issues were a lot to add to the ones she'd brought to the ranch. An escaped convict and her ex's father who seemed determined to get his hand on his grandson. Her plan was turning out to contain a myriad of complications.

And perhaps danger.

Jonah Burke definitely wasn't a man she wanted to tangle with on top of everything else.

She heard the sound behind her and automatically reached for her gun. Collena tried to force herself to calm down. After all, Millie had walked in earlier without knocking. Maybe the woman had returned.

But this didn't feel right.

Collena felt a too-familiar shiver go down her spine. A cop's shiver. A warning that she was in the presence of danger.

The doorknob turned again. Not gently. An almost frantic gesture.

"Who is it?" Collena called out.

No one answered.

With her heart in her throat, her blood pumping and with her gun gripped in her hand, Collena threw open the door.

No one was there. And the corridor was empty. Well, empty except for the yellowy newspaper that was lying on the floor near her feet.

While keeping watch around her, she stooped and picked up the *Greer Herald*. It wasn't the weekly edition. It wasn't even recent.

The date indicated it was five years old.

During the background check she'd done on Dylan, Collena had yet to see anything from the *Greer Herald*. The small newspaper wasn't electronically stored, nor had there been any online copies. Since both the newspaper office and the town library had closed early for the Thanksgiving holiday, she hadn't been able to read any back issues.

Confused as to why someone would leave something like that outside the guest-room door, Collena glanced at the front page. The lead story was the sheriff's investigation into Abigail Greer's death.

Dylan's sister.

According to the article, there had been no witnesses to

the suspicious car fire that'd killed Abigail. Collena kept reading, scanning through the lengthy article that detailed the specifics of what remained of the vehicle.

And then she realized someone had highlighted a line near the end of the newspaper report.

"Dylan Greer has been brought in for questioning and is considered a suspect in his sister's and fiancée's deaths."

Chapter Seven

This was not the quiet, relaxing Thanksgiving dinner that Dylan had planned.

The table was filled with all the traditional foods that he'd requested Ina make—roasted turkey with all the trimmings, mashed potatoes, gravy and three vegetable dishes.

Everything looked perfect. It probably tasted good, too, but he doubted anyone at the table, other than Deputy Burke, knew that firsthand. Ruth, Millie, Ina, Hank, the handyman, and even Dylan himself were picking at their food and trying to avoid direct eye contact with anyone else.

Collena wasn't even making an attempt to eat, and Dylan didn't think it was his imagination that she seemed leery of him.

The sole bright spot was Adam.

He sat in his high chair eating peas and tiny bits of turkey. Each bite seemed to amuse him, because he babbled and grinned at Dylan. Despite the trouble of the day, Dylan had no choice but to smile back at the little boy. Those smiles were welcome reminders that he was well worth fighting for.

Dylan spotted Collena smiling, too, and Adam seemed pleased that he had someone else's attention. He offered Collena a pea that was pinched between his tiny thumb and forefinger, and Collena got up to take the offer.

Adam giggled when Collena ate the pea from his fingers.

"You two sure look an awful lot alike," Jonah commented. He shoveled another forkful of mashed potatoes into his mouth.

For such a simple comment, it certainly caused a reaction. Everyone stopped, as if waiting to see how Dylan would respond to that. Then, seconds later, Ruth tossed her silverware onto her plate. It made a loud clanging sound.

"Adam's tired," Ruth announced, standing. "It's time for me to get him ready for bed."

Collena looked at Dylan. "Can't he stay up just a little longer?" There was a definite motherly plea in her voice. Just as there was a back-me-up plea in Ruth's eyes.

And that's when Dylan knew he had to put a stop to this.

First, he motioned for Ruth and Collena to sit down, and because he was positive he would need it, he finished off his glass of wine.

"Collena is Adam's birth mother," he started, making brief eye contact with everyone at the table. "Someone stole Adam from her, and Collena's spent all these months looking for him." He had to pause a moment. "The adoption was probably illegal."

No one seemed shocked by that revelation, which meant it'd likely been the topic of house gossip all afternoon.

"You didn't know it was illegal," Millie declared. "The judge will understand that. You won't lose Adam."

Dylan wasn't so certain of that.

"What about Curtis Reese?" Jonah asked. "What's he got to do with any of this?"

"He's Adam's grandfather," Collena answered before Dylan could.

Dylan added to the explanation. "And he plans to fight both Collena and me for custody of Adam."

Now, that caused a reaction. Jonah stopped eating and stared openmouthed at Dylan. Millie flattened her hand over her chest and frantically shook her head. Ruth went ash pale and slowly sank back onto her seat.

"He can't take Adam," Millie said practically in a whisper.

Dylan nodded. "Collena and I have a plan to stop that from happening." That also got everyone's attention. Dylan figured he was going to get more than their attention with what he had to say next. "Collena and I have decided to join forces to fight Reese. And the best way for us to do that is get married and have me legally adopt Adam."

"Married?" Millie and Ruth said in unison.

Hank and Ina apparently decided it was a good time to go check on dessert. He didn't blame them. Dylan waited until they were out of the room before he continued.

"Together Collena and I can make a stronger case for custody," he added.

Millie stood. "But marriage?"

Dylan nodded again. "I've gone through all the options, and this is the best one for fighting Reese off."

"So, this would strictly be a marriage of convenience?" Jonah asked while still chewing his food. Despite what had to be a shocking conversation, it'd only deterred Jonah from eating for a few seconds.

"Yes." And Dylan hoped they all understood that. After

what'd happened to the other women he'd loved, he wanted to make it crystal clear that he didn't care for Collena.

That was the only way he could save her from the fate of the other women. Even then, it was still a risk. This might open old wounds that he never wanted open. Now, if he could only figure out whose *wounds* it was that had made his life a living hell.

"There has to be another way," Ruth declared. "You can't marry her, Dylan. She could take Adam and run."

"She can try to do that even if we're not married," Dylan pointed out. "Collena is Adam's mother. I have no legal or moral right to try to cut her out of Adam's life."

Ruth stared at him, and there were tears in her eyes. "Adam's tired," she repeated. "It's time for me to get him ready for bed."

Collena got up again, as well. "I want to go with him so I can say good-night."

Ruth took off the high-chair tray, picked up Adam and turned around to face Collena. "Give the baby some time. You can't force motherhood on him."

With that, Ruth took Adam out of the room.

Dylan considered going after her, to remind Ruth that while she was a member of the family, she couldn't shut out Collena, but he decided they could all use a little breathing space. Besides, with their late start on the Thanksgiving dinner, it really was Adam's bedtime.

"I'll have to excuse myself from the table, too," Millie said. "I'm not feeling well."

Jonah smiled at Collena. "You sure know how to clear a table."

That brought Dylan to his feet. He was about to give Jonah a piece of his mind, but Collena stopped him.

"Don't," she whispered. "It's not worth it." She stood and placed her napkin beside her plate. "If you don't mind, I need to get some rest. It's been a long day."

Dylan shot Jonah a nasty glare and headed after her. Collena was in the corridor, and she was already practically running in the direction of her guest room.

"Wait," he called out to her.

She didn't exactly wait, but she did slow down so he could catch up with her. "I really am tired," she told him.

"I don't doubt that." Dylan caught her arm and turned her around to face him.

He'd had some good ideas in his life, but that wasn't one of them. When he whirled her around, she practically landed against him. So close they were nearly touching. He saw the stark fatigue in her eyes. The worry lines on her forehead. The too-pale skin.

But he also took in her scent. Not warm, exactly. But inviting. He was attracted to her in the most basic way that a man could be attracted to a woman.

Collena was beautiful. And she had both a toughness and a fragileness about her. The kind of woman who could take care of herself but was still vulnerable beneath. He was a sucker for a strong woman, but his attraction went up a significant notch when there was vulnerability involved.

"Well?" Collena prompted. She took a step back. It didn't help. She was still close enough that her scent was playing havoc with his senses.

"I apologize for Ruth's comment," Dylan said, forcing himself to speak.

"No need. I didn't think for one minute that fitting into your life would be easy. And the truth is, I'll try to stay out of their way—and yours—as much as possible."

He studied her, specifically her defensive posture. She'd folded her arms over her chest and was leaning away from him. Definitely defensive.

"Okay, what's this all about?" he asked. He motioned toward her folded arms.

To her credit, she didn't say, *What do you mean?* Nor did she deny that something was wrong. "Earlier today someone left a newspaper outside my door."

Though that didn't seem serious, Dylan wasn't ready to shrug just yet. A lot of crazy things had happened. "What newspaper?"

Collena opened the door to her room and, without turning on the light, went inside. Several moments later, she returned with the article in question. One glance at it, and Dylan didn't have to ask any more questions about what it was. He knew. It was *the* story that had implicated him in the deaths of his sister and fiancée.

"I didn't kill them," Dylan said simply.

Collena looked him straight in the eyes. "I believe you."

He was so surprised by her adamant vote of confidence that it took him a moment to respond. "Then why did that article upset you?"

"Because first of all, I don't know who left it for me. Or why. Maybe the person was trying to make me run in the other direction. But I won't run," she insisted.

No, he didn't think she would. But Dylan did want to know the answer to her questions. Who had left it? Obviously someone on his staff. Or maybe Jonah. He was in the house, too. And as for why, maybe this was a little gaslighting, an attempt to make Collena feel unwelcome.

And unsafe.

Oh, yes. He'd question everyone in the house, and he'd get to the bottom of this.

"I also think Curtis Reese might try to use this article against us," Collena added.

Of course. Dylan should have thought of that. Even though there'd been no evidence against him and even though he was never a solid suspect, there had been questions and gossip about his innocence. Those questions had been raised in that particular story in the *Greer Herald.*

"I can't make that article go away," Dylan explained. He took the newspaper from her and tucked it under his arm. "But I can have my lawyer negate it by pointing out that I was never charged with a crime."

"Still…" She groaned softly and leaned against the wall. "Curtis already has so much ammunition. That's why I proposed."

"I know. And it's a good idea."

She blinked.

He blinked, too. "Did I just say that?"

The smile that curved her mouth was born of pure irony and frustration. "It might take a decade or two before your staff believes it's a good idea."

"They'll get used to it, because they won't have a choice. I'm not losing Adam, and if this marriage can stop that from happening, then we need to say 'I do' as soon as possible."

"How soon is that?" she asked.

Dylan couldn't believe he was about to say this, either. "I plan to call the county clerk tonight at his home. He's an old friend. I want him to expedite the licensing process, and if all goes well, I think I can have everything arranged for this weekend."

She blinked again. "That soon?"

He heard the doubts in her voice and knew they'd be in his voice, as well. "Curtis Reese will probably be filing his custody petition as early as tomorrow morning."

Collena drew in a hard breath. "You're right. We should do this as soon as the county clerk has the license." She paused. "You'll tell Ruth and the others about the hasty wedding plans?"

"Yes." Though he knew that wouldn't be a pleasant conversation. Nor would the other chat he'd have to have with Adam's nanny. "I'm not going to let Ruth cut you out of Adam's life."

Collena shook her head. "I wouldn't let that happen anyway." She touched her index finger to her mouth. "I am concerned though about Ruth being under the care of a therapist."

Ah, so she'd learned that. "She is. Millie, too. My sister's death sent them both into emotional tailspins. Don't worry though, it doesn't affect how they interact with Adam. They both love him, and they wouldn't do anything to hurt him. I'd stake my life on that."

"I can see they love him," Collena admitted. "But I can also see that Ruth is going to make it very difficult for me. She won't succeed. I've worked too hard to find Adam to allow anyone to stop me from being his mother."

Even though she probably hadn't meant that as a challenge or an order, it made Dylan feel a little defensive. He had to remind himself—again—that he couldn't have an adversarial relationship with Collena. But that did bring him to another question.

Just what kind of relationship would this really be?

They'd both already established that it was to be a marriage of convenience, but he certainly couldn't deny the attraction he felt for her.

Was it one-sided?

Dylan studied her. They were still close, and they seemed to get a whole lot closer when her eyes came to his. He saw it then. The heat. He felt it, too. And knew this wasn't a good thing.

Dylan chose his words carefully. "There's this connection between us," he admitted.

She nodded. "Conflict at first sight."

"It's not all conflict, and that's the problem."

Her stare intensified before she mumbled something under her breath and looked away. "We feel this way because we're comrades of sorts. We've made a pact not to lose custody of Adam."

"That's part of it, I'm sure. But the other part is that we're physically attracted to each other," he added. "Don't deny it."

"I wasn't planning to. Yes, it exists. That doesn't mean we have to act on it. In fact, acting on it could cause problems for us in other areas."

"You're right," Dylan admitted. "There's that unresolved issue of my past relationships. Besides, sex would complicate things."

No more leaning against the wall. She practically snapped to attention. "Who said anything about sex?"

He lifted his eyebrow.

Just like that, her body relaxed, and Collena shrugged. "Attraction leads to sex—point taken. It can't happen though."

"I'm sure you're right, but if this attraction gets any

stronger, we might have trouble remembering why it'd be a bad idea."

"It'd be bad because it would get in the way of what we both want, being the best possible parents to Adam."

He nodded. "That's a good argument."

But it didn't stop a curl of heat from making its way through his body. It was just basic lust, he repeated to himself, intensified because of the camaraderie and because it'd been too long since he'd been with a woman.

Way too long.

His body just wouldn't let him forget that.

Nor would it let him forget that judging from the look in Collena's eyes, she was engaged in the same battle he was.

"My, isn't this cozy?" Dylan heard someone ask.

He looked over his shoulder and saw Jonah making his way toward them. The deputy had obviously noticed the proximity of Collena and him, because Jonah was grinning as if he'd just caught them raiding the cookie jar.

"Did I interrupt anything?" Jonah asked.

"Nothing that we care to share with you," Dylan fired back.

That caused Jonah's nostrils to flare. The man stopped just several inches away from them. "You just don't learn, do you, Dylan?"

"What's that supposed to mean?"

"You don't have a real good track record with women, now, do you? I seem to recall the last one you got engaged to was killed in that car fire."

Dylan shifted his posture and glared at Jonah. "Is that some kind of threat?"

Jonah held up his hands in mock surrender, and he

chuckled. "Not from me." The jovial expression quickly faded, and the look in the deputy's eyes turned dark. "But even you can't deny that you've got a problem. My advice? Watch your back and hers. I don't want to be investigating another suspicious death or two."

With that, Jonah strolled away in the direction of the other guest room.

The curl of heat was quickly replaced with anger, and followed by the realization that while Jonah was an SOB, he was also right.

Dylan *did* need to watch Collena's back.

In his attempt to keep custody of Adam, he couldn't endanger Collena's life.

It was time to reopen some of his own personal wounds and take another hard look at what'd happened years ago.

"Jonah obviously doesn't want to see you happy," Collena said. She waited until Jonah was in his room before she continued. "I learned some things about him."

"That he was stalking my sister right before she was killed." Dylan nodded. "I believe it's true, though Jonah has denied it. He said it was all a misunderstanding, that he thought my sister was truly interested in him."

"He was also dating Millie at the time."

"You've done your homework." And Dylan couldn't fault her for it. He was investigating her and her friends, as well. "Yes, they were dating, but I think Jonah was doing that only to make my sister jealous. It might have worked if Abigail had had any feelings for Jonah. But she didn't."

Collena folded her arms over her chest. "I have to ask— do you think Jonah could have had something to do with your sister's death?"

He didn't have to think long about his answer. "I honestly don't know. If he did, he certainly hid his guilt."

"Some people don't feel guilt." Collena glanced down the hall at Jonah's room and scrubbed her hand over the back of her neck. "I should get some rest. You, too. We have a long day ahead of us."

He couldn't dispute that, but after the conversation they'd just had about Jonah, Dylan didn't want to take any chances. "This is probably overkill since you're a former cop, but I'd like to check your room."

Her eyes widened. "You think…" But she didn't finish that. She merely stepped aside so that Dylan could go in.

He didn't waste any time. He turned on the lights, and with Collena trailing right behind him, he checked first the sitting room and then the adjoining bedroom suite.

Nothing seemed out of the ordinary.

Dylan turned toward her. "Lock your door tonight."

"I intend to. And I have my gun."

He nodded, though he hated the idea that Collena might ever have to use it. In fact, he had to believe there'd be no need to use it. He'd done everything possible to create the safest environment for Adam, and he had to trust that all his security measures would be enough.

However, first thing in the morning, he was getting Jonah out of there, and he would turn on the corridor security cameras to make sure Jonah didn't leave his room. In addition, he'd set the security system in the nursery so that no one could sneak in there.

Dylan considered asking Collena if she wanted him to stay in her suite with her. He briefly considered it anyway. But another look at her reminded him that would be a really bad idea.

Besides, he wasn't even certain there was a threat.

The newspaper could have been Millie or Ruth's way of trying to make Collena want to run in the other direction. And if so, they wouldn't get away with it. If he found out they were behind this, there'd be hell to pay. He'd make it clear to both women that he wasn't going to let them do this to Collena.

Dylan and she walked back into the sitting room. That's when he noticed the message light blinking on the phone. "Someone must have called you."

Collena looked in the direction of the phone and stared at the red blinking light. "No one I know has that number. All my calls having been coming through my cell."

That put a new knot in his stomach. Still, the most logical answer was that it was a wrong number. Hoping that was true, Dylan went to the phone and punched the button.

It was several moments before he heard any sound. First, there was static. Lots of it. The line crackled and hissed as if the connection was really bad.

Then, there was the voice.

"Collena," the person said through the hiss and static. The voice was muted.

No, not muted.

Disguised.

The caller had something over his or her mouth.

Collena moved closer, until they were side-by-side, and they continued to stare at the phone. Waiting.

"Collena," the voice repeated. "Are you ready to die?"

Chapter Eight

Collena had experienced one of the longest nights of her life, and she wasn't holding out any hope that the day after would be any easier.

With the threatening phone call, the newspaper appearing outside her door, Curtis Reese's custody threat and Rodney Harmon's escape from jail, her stress and anxiety levels were sky-high.

What made everything tolerable was Adam.

Much to Ruth's disapproval, Collena had insisted that she feed her son breakfast. Then, she bathed Adam. The process hadn't gone perfectly, especially with Ruth shadowing her every move, but Collena ignored the woman and just enjoyed her first precious moments of motherhood.

There would be lots more of these moments.

And it would take more than a threatening call to put her off.

Collena dressed Adam in denim overalls, brushed his hair and carried him into the playroom so they could have some reading time.

Ruth followed her.

"You're getting him out of his morning routine," Ruth complained.

Collena considered ignoring her, but she decided it was time to get things straight. Ruth's criticisms had been going on for hours, and she didn't want it to continue. "Adam's my son," Collena stated firmly. "I'm going to raise him. And right now, I'm going to read him a book."

Ruth pulled back her shoulders. "You're trying to cut me out of his life."

"No, I'm not. Dylan hired you, so he obviously believes you're a good nanny." At least she hoped that was true, that Ruth wasn't still around simply because she'd become a fixture at the ranch. "I have no intentions of cutting you out of Adam's life. But I won't have you trying to do the same to me."

Ruth's shoulders relaxed a bit, and after several snail-crawling moments, she gave a crisp nod. "I'll give you two some time to read," she said as if it were a massive concession. Which for her, it probably was. And then the woman quietly left the room.

"Alone at last," Collena mumbled.

She sat on the floor, put Adam right next to her and selected a book from the large stack. Adam cocked his head to the side, studying her, before he climbed into Collena's lap. It was an amazing feeling, and it was several moments before Collena could find her voice so she could read to her child. However, she barely made it through the first page before someone opened the door.

It was Dylan.

As much as Collena hated to have her time with Adam interrupted, she wanted to see Dylan, as well, so she could find out what progress he'd made on the threatening phone call and Curtis's custody petition.

And much to her displeasure, she realized she also wanted to see him just for the sake of seeing him.

She certainly got an eyeful.

He wore faded jeans that hugged his well-toned lower body and a white shirt that did the same for his equally well toned torso. He hadn't shaved and had rather hot-looking desperado stubble.

"You found out who made that call?" Collena asked, forcing herself to get her mind back on business and off Dylan's body.

He kept his expression pleasant, no doubt for Adam's sake, and came and sat on the floor next to them. Adam immediately left Collena's lap for his, and the child gave Dylan a sloppy kiss on the cheek. Dylan returned the kiss.

"There are private lines in both guest rooms where you and Jonah were staying," Dylan explained while he played patty-cake with Adam. "Both numbers are listed so they'd be easy for anyone to get them. And there was an identical message on the machine in Jonah's room."

Collena processed that info. "So, the call could have come from anyone who knew I was staying here. Anyone, including Curtis Reese or Rodney Harmon." It sickened her to think of a man like Harmon having any contact with the ranch.

She wanted him far away from Adam.

"I tried to have the call traced, of course," Dylan continued. "But it came from a prepaid cell phone."

Collena knew what that meant. The call wouldn't be traceable. The threat was a dead end because, in addition to Rodney Harmon or Curtis Reese, Ruth or Millie could have made the call. For that matter, Jonah could have, as well. The message on the phone in his guest room could have been a ruse to throw suspicion off him.

"You look tired," Dylan said. He reached out and slid his finger over her cheek to push away a lock of hair that had strayed from her ponytail. His touch was warm. And comforting.

"You look tired, too. Probably because you stayed outside my door all night."

He nodded and seemed a little surprised that she'd known that little detail. "Since the nursery's at the end of that particular hall, I figured I could keep an eye on both Adam and you."

"Thank you for that. For Adam's sake. But since I have my gun, I feel safe."

That was a lie, but Collena didn't want him to think she was a wuss. Dylan had enough to worry about without adding her to his list.

Dylan handed Adam a toy dog. "Curtis Reese filed the custody motion this morning."

Collena had been expecting him to say that, but it still hit her hard. It took her a moment to gather her breath. "And what about Rodney Harmon? I don't suppose the police have found him?"

"Not yet. But I hired a couple of P.I.s to look for him, as well."

That was a start, and she had to remind herself that Dylan had an excellent security system at the ranch. No, it hadn't prevented that troubling call, but it would probably stop an intruder from breaking in. After all, he'd detected her with ease when she was by the birthing stables. Now that they knew Rodney Harmon was on the loose, Dylan had no doubt beefed up security even more.

Plus, he'd slept outside her door.

Collena didn't want to be touched by that.

But she was.

"There's nothing new on your car," he continued. He divided his attention between Adam and her. "The fire chief is still thinking it was an electrical problem, but he's going to continue to investigate."

Collena hoped it was an electrical fire that hadn't been spurred by human's means. It was far better than the alternative, but considering that phone call, the car and the call could have been attempts to run her out of town.

"Did anyone on the staff know about the newspaper left outside my door?" she asked.

"Everyone denied putting it there." He scrubbed his hand over his face. "Obviously, someone is lying."

Obviously. "If the newspaper was only meant to unnerve me, I can live with that." Collena stopped and tried to decide the best way to continue. But Dylan had no trouble picking up on where this conversation was going.

"You think this has something to do with the deaths of my sister and fiancée. And the other attacks," he added.

She drew back her shoulders. "What other attacks?"

Dylan shrugged, but there was nothing casual about the gesture. "I figured you'd come across that in the background check."

"I didn't." And Collena braced herself for the worst. Thankfully, Adam helped soften the impact. The little boy's laughter broke the tension building inside Collena.

"It started when I was seventeen. My high school girlfriend was assaulted. Someone clubbed her when she was getting into her car one night. She wasn't able to get a look at her attacker because the assault happened from behind."

Oh, mercy. Collena could only hold her breath while Dylan continued.

"Then, when I was in college, a woman I dated was also beaten."

"I take it the only thing these women, your fiancée and your sister, had in common was…you?" she asked.

"Yes. And I know what you're thinking—did someone I know commit these crimes."

"You mean, Deputy Burke?" She didn't wait for him to confirm that. "He certainly seems capable of doing something malicious. I don't know about murder though."

Dylan lifted his shoulder. "Maybe the fires weren't meant to kill them."

She considered that. She also considered something else. "What if it was someone else connected to you, someone who works for you?"

He stayed quiet a moment. "I had to consider that, but then I dismissed it. The only people who were around for all the incidents were Millie, Ruth and Hank, the handyman."

Collena tried not to make the tone of her next question sound confrontational. "Both Millie and Ruth are under care of a therapist. Maybe one of them is, uh, well, a little unbalanced."

Dylan looked neither surprised, nor upset with the suggestion. "Anything is possible. But I just don't see it. Ruth's been a great nanny, and Millie practically runs the household. If either of them is a sociopath with killer tendencies, it hasn't shown up in any behavior or any incident here at the ranch."

"Maybe because you've stopped dating and therefore

you've stopped giving one of them a reason to do something violent."

He stared at her. Rather than getting angry about that theory, he actually seemed thoughtful before he shook his head. "Ruth loves me like her own son. I'm sure of that. I'm also sure that she wants me to be happy."

Collena wasn't so certain of that at all. "And what about Millie?"

Another headshake. "She's not romantically obsessed with me. She sees other men. Heck, she was engaged to a guy from San Antonio just last year, but things didn't work out between them."

"Well, that leaves Hank, and I'm not about to accuse a seventysomething-year-old man of murder and assault." She paused. "Unless you think there's a reason to accuse him."

"No reason at all. My dad died when I was a kid, and Hank stepped up to do all the things that a dad normally would have done. He was also a huge help to my mom when it came to running the business. When she died of breast cancer eight years ago, Hank took it as hard as I did."

So, Hank was family. Not that being family was a good enough reason to remove him from a list of suspects.

"Hank is Ruth's father and Millie's grandfather," Dylan added.

"I didn't know that." She wondered if that bit of information was important. "I didn't investigate him before I came to the ranch."

"All three—Millie, Ruth and Hank—are Sayers. Ruth was never married to Millie's father, so that's why they have the same surname." Dylan looked at her again. "Do you want me to have them move out for a while?"

Collena wanted to jump at the chance for that to happen. But it wasn't fair. Not to them. Nor was it fair to Adam. Besides, Dylan was right. There were no solid indications that the women wanted to prevent him from being happy in love.

However, she couldn't say the same for Jonah.

She really needed to do some more digging into his past.

"What about the roads?" Collena asked. It was obviously time for a change of subject. The mood was positively gloomy. "Are they still impassable?"

Dylan shook his head. "They've been plowed."

"Does that mean Jonah is on his way home?"

"He left about an hour ago."

Well, that was something to celebrate, but Dylan didn't look in a celebratory mood. And that brought her to something she should have already suggested. "Do you want me to move to a hotel?"

"Absolutely not. We only have one hotel in town, and Curtis Reese is staying there."

"Right." She definitely didn't want to be near him.

"Besides, it's too risky for you to leave," Dylan added.

"You mean, too risky because of Rodney Harmon?" Collena knew he couldn't verify that Rodney was the only risk, but she wanted to know if he was ready to admit that someone in his household might have been responsible for the car fire and the threatening call.

"Rodney Harmon. Curtis Reese," he verified. "Plus, there's the wedding."

Yes. That.

Despite all the other thoughts and fears that'd clogged her brain and prevented her from sleeping, Collena hadn't been able to get the wedding off her mind.

When she'd first come up with the marriage plan, it'd seemed like a solid idea, but now she was having her doubts. But she didn't have another choice. Without being a married couple, they wouldn't be able to put up a strong fight to stop Curtis Reese.

Dylan scraped his thumbnail over the book that she'd laid next to her. "I've already arranged for the marriage license. The county clerk went to his office despite the holiday and expedited everything. And with the roads clear, the justice of the peace should be able to get here without any trouble. We'll be able to do this soon."

"How soon is soon?" she asked.

He cleared his throat. "This afternoon."

Of course, she'd known that Dylan intended to move quickly, but she certainly hadn't anticipated they would say *I do* in mere hours.

"You're having second thoughts," he said.

Second, third and fourth. She only hoped she wasn't inviting even more danger for all of them by becoming Mrs. Dylan Greer.

DYLAN TOOK OUT his gun from the desk drawer and slipped it in the leather shoulder holster hidden beneath his suit coat. He doubted many men carried a gun on their wedding day, but this wasn't any normal wedding day.

There was a killer on the loose.

And a cold-case killer who might try to make a return visit.

This obviously wouldn't be a dream-come-true wedding. But he had to stay focused on Adam. The wedding would help him keep custody.

He hoped.

There was a tap at the door, and Dylan figured that the justice of peace had arrived. So, it was time. Which was good because his doubts were growing by leaps and bounds. It was best to get this over before he did something stupid such as change his mind.

"Come in," he offered.

The door opened, and Millie stepped inside. "I want to talk to you."

Oh, man. He didn't like the sound of that, and he didn't have to guess what she wanted to discuss. "Is the J.P. here yet?" Because if so, their conversation would have to wait.

"No. He's just called. He's running a little late." Millie shut the door behind her and leaned against it as if blocking his path. "Dylan, are you sure about going through with this wedding?"

He buttoned his jacket so no one would be able to see his gun. "I want to keep custody of Adam."

"There has to be another way."

Since her comment had a hint of desperation to it, Dylan couldn't help but think back to the conversation he'd had with Collena that morning. Was Millie obsessed with him in some way? He'd known Millie all her life, since they were practically the same age. He was thirty-two—Millie, thirty-one. They'd been raised together, more like brother and sister than the nanny's daughter and the ranch owner's son. He studied her eyes, her expression, even her body language, but the only thing he saw was an old friend concerned about his well-being.

Of course, people wore masks.

"You don't know Collena," Millie continued. "You could wait and see what Curtis Reese is going to do. Who knows, he might change his mind and withdraw his petition for custody."

"You know something I don't?" Dylan asked.

"No. But people do that. They change. They do what's right. He might decide that Adam is better off with you."

"I'm not going to hold my breath waiting for that," Dylan mumbled. He went to the closet and rifled through one of the dresser drawers until he found something he rarely wore—his cuff links. It took him a few moments to get them into place.

When he turned around, Millie was right in front of him. Mere inches away.

Staring at him.

"Please," she said, trying to blink back tears. She wasn't successful. "Don't do this."

Dylan got a really bad feeling about her reaction. He stepped out of the closet. "What's this all about?"

"I'm scared," she whispered. Her bottom lip began to tremble. "What if this time the killer goes after you? What if it's your car that catches on fire? What if you're the next one who dies?"

As chilling as that was, Dylan actually relaxed a bit at the realization that it could happen. Because he'd much rather a killer come after him than Collena or Adam. Besides, he welcomed such a confrontation. He'd wanted to confront this SOB for years.

There was another knock at the door, followed by Hank's somber voice. "The justice of the peace is here," he announced. "Everybody's gathering in the family room, just like you wanted."

That was Dylan's cue to get moving. First though, he

used his thumb to wipe the tears off Millie's cheek. "Everything will be okay," he promised.

And he would do everything humanly possible to make sure he kept that promise.

With Millie by his side, Dylan went into the corridor where Hank was waiting. Hank shot him a questioning glance, and even though the man didn't voice his objection to these nuptials, the argument was there in the depths of his aged eyes.

Dylan ignored it but encountered more questioning stares as soon as he stepped into the family room and saw Ruth. The nanny was standing just inside the arched double doorway. She cast her daughter a glance, and Millie shook her head, apparently letting her mother know that she had not succeeded in talking him out of this.

With Hank, Millie, Ruth and even the sour-looking justice of the peace, the energy in the family room was tense.

Until he spotted Collena.

Holding Adam in her arms, she stood by the floor-to-ceiling white limestone fireplace, a mesquite fire flickering in the hearth. Collena wore a straight-cut pale green dress that landed just above her knees. Adam wore a dark blue one-piece corduroy suit.

Unlike the others, Adam wasn't somber. He was playing a modified peekaboo game with Collena. Collena was reciprocating with the game, but Dylan figured her efforts were an attempt to cover her nerves.

Then, she turned and looked at him.

Dylan hadn't anticipated the reaction he would have when he saw her face. She wasn't so pale this afternoon. There was a peachy tone to her skin, and that color was deepened on her mouth.

For just a moment, he forgot the marriage was a pretense.

For just a moment, he forgot how to breathe.

Man, Collena was beautiful. Definitely not the fragile pale waif that had fainted outside the stables. This was a woman with warmth, substance, and his gut reaction was intensified by the fact that she held his son so lovingly in her arms.

He went to her, and Collena leaned in to whisper in his ear. "You look ready for the firing squad," she joked.

Dylan appreciated her attempt to keep things light, but the whisper and even the joke felt too intimate. A glance around the room told him that the others had interpreted it as intimate, as well.

That couldn't happen.

He wasn't ready to concede that Hank, Millie or Ruth was a cold-blooded killer, but all three could gossip. If word got out that he was indeed attracted to his soon-to-be wife, then the killer might be tempted to come out of hiding. And go after not him but Collena. It was best to keep his lust hidden away, and that hiding started right here, right now. Then he could make sure the word got out that this was a marriage of convenience, just in case the killer thought this was real.

"Let's get this done," Dylan said to Martin Caldwell, the J.P. The short, round-bellied man gave his thick bifocals an adjustment and opened a leather folder that contained the license and other paperwork.

The J.P. glanced at both of them from over the top of his glasses. "Do you, Dylan Greer, and you, Collena Drake, assent to a mutual agreement to take each other as marital spouses?"

There it was. Dry as dust. Practically sterile. Just what Dylan had requested.

"I do," Dylan quickly answered.

Collena followed suit. "I do."

Adam tried to repeat the two words, his attempt causing them to smile. Again, it felt intimate.

"Will you exchange rings?" the J.P. asked.

"No," he and Collena said in unison. No ring. No symbol that this was a real marriage.

The J.P. glanced around the room. "Are there any objections to this union?"

With the most intense glare he could manage, Dylan dared them to object. All three stayed quiet.

"Then, I, Martin Caldwell, justice of the peace in the state of Texas, act in my official capacity in pronouncing you to be husband and wife." He looked at Dylan. "If you're going to kiss her, now's the time to do it."

"No kiss," Dylan mumbled. Though it suddenly seemed like something he wanted to do. He pushed that desire aside.

Ruth started crying. Millie stared at them as if they'd done the most horrific thing she'd ever witnessed. Hank just stared at the window.

Dylan glanced at Collena to see how she was holding up. She, too, looked a little shell-shocked, but he couldn't soothe her, not even in a friendly sort of way. He didn't want his feelings misinterpreted.

"Jonah's back," Hank announced. He left the window and headed for the front door to let the deputy in.

Collena groaned softly.

Dylan shared her sentiment. He thanked the justice of

the peace, handed him some cash, and then he and Collena signed the marriage license.

With each stroke of the pen, Dylan couldn't help but wonder if he'd sealed their fate.

The J.P. headed out just as Jonah entered the family room.

"This better be important," Dylan commented.

Jonah didn't even acknowledge that he'd just walked in on a wedding ceremony. Or maybe, with the mood in the room, he simply wasn't aware of it. "Don't look at me like that," Jonah snarled. "You think I enjoy coming back out here? I don't. This is business."

Dylan was afraid of that, and he knew that if the business required a personal trip to the ranch, it couldn't be good news.

"First of all, Curtis Reese is staying at the hotel in town. Y'all already know that. But what you don't know is that he filed a harassment complaint against the two of you because someone left a threatening message on the phone in his room."

"You mean, a message like the one left on the two guest-room phones?" Collena asked.

"Identical," Jonah confirmed. "Obviously, someone had too much time on their hands."

Dylan hoped that was all there was to it. A prank. But he didn't believe that.

Dylan's breath streamed out in frustration. "You drove out here to tell us this?"

"No. I drove out here because our fax machine's on the fritz, and the sheriff said that Collena needs to take a look at these two pictures right away."

Collena took the first photo that Jonah handed her, and both she and Dylan studied the grainy shot. Even with the lack of clarity, Dylan had no trouble seeing the tall, dark-haired man in the center of the photo.

"The camera in the ATM of the bank in town snapped the pictures," Jonah explained. "The bank manager saw 'em this morning and got suspicious since he'd never seen the man before. So, how about it, Collena, do you recognize him?"

She nodded. Then nodded again. The motion was choppy, as was her breath. "That's Rodney Harmon."

Dylan cursed. That meant the escaped felon was close. Too close. And they didn't need this complication on top of everything else.

"You're sure that's Harmon?" Jonah asked Collena.

"Positive."

Jonah looked past her and fixed his attention on Dylan. "Harmon was obviously in town just a few hours ago. I'm betting he's still there."

That meant they had a killer bearing down on them. "You said there were two pictures?"

"Yeah." Jonah didn't add anything for several seconds. Then he took the second photo from beneath his arm and gave it to Collena.

It was another picture of Rodney Harmon, but this one was clearer because he was closer to the ATM camera. In fact, the man was staring directly into the camera as if he had known this recorded image would make its way to Collena.

And it had.

In his hands, Rodney Harmon was holding up a hand-scrawled cardboard sign that was as clear as the sneer on the man's face. The words on the sign hit Dylan like a fist.

"Collena, are you ready to die?"

Chapter Nine

Years earlier, before her idea of romance had turned sour, Collena had often dreamed of her wedding night. What she hadn't included in that dream was a loveless marriage and a monster out to kill her.

Added to that, both the groom and she were armed with semiautomatics and would be indefinitely, until the danger had passed.

However, there were some pluses to this particular wedding night. Well, one anyway. She and Dylan were going to spend the night in the nursery alongside Adam. With Rodney Harmon's latest death threat and with the uncertain motives of those in Dylan's household, it seemed the reasonable and cautious thing to do.

Unfortunately, when they had come up with the sleeping arrangement, Collena had failed to grasp the full impact of staying in the same room with Dylan. Alone, with a sleeping toddler.

Close quarters probably weren't a bright idea with the attraction brewing between them. Still, there weren't many options, and keeping Adam safe was their top priority.

"I had this moved from one of the guest rooms," Dylan

whispered as he motioned toward the double bed with the wrought iron headboard. "Let's hope it's comfortable."

Collena eyed the bed and the stack of bedding they'd taken from the linen closet. Then, she eyed Dylan in his hot jeans and a chest-hugging black tee. Nope. Neither the bed, nor her husband would make this situation comfortable.

"I doubt I'll get much sleep anyway." Collena kept her voice as soft as possible so she wouldn't wake Adam. Her little boy had had a long day and needed his rest.

"Try," Dylan insisted. "Neither of us will be much good to Adam if we're dead tired."

She nodded because he was right. That didn't mean, however, that sleep was going to happen.

Especially if they were in the same bed.

Since they hadn't specifically discussed the sleeping arrangements, Collena stood there and waited to see what Dylan planned to do. From across the mattress, her eyes met his. Even in the dimly lit room, she could see what he was thinking.

There was heat stirring in those eyes. Thankfully, there was also concern. Maybe the concern would win out.

"I can sleep on the floor," he suggested.

"Or we can put pillows between us."

Silence followed, a long, uncomfortable silence where they just stared at each other. "Pillows," he finally agreed after glancing at the floor.

Collena picked up the sheet, unfolded it, and they began to make the bed. "The security company delivered extra motion-activated monitors this afternoon like the one over there," he explained, hitching his thumb at the thin monitor mounted on the wall near Adam's changing table. "They'll pick up movement outside the house. I figured it'd help if everyone in the house was keeping an eye on the grounds."

Yes, it would help. Unless someone in the house was the one to watch for. "And you said something about having someone monitor the security system?"

"I hired a pair of P.I.s who'll be on monitor duty and act as backup if we need it. They're working out of my office for now, but tomorrow, they'll move into the other guest room just in case this situation lasts for a while."

In other words if Rodney Harmon stormed onto the ranch with guns blazing, there'd be at least four of them to stop him. She hoped that was enough, because Collena was a hundred-percent certain that Harmon would try to come after her.

It was only a matter of time.

Unless the cops could catch him first.

Collena gave Adam a soft kiss on the cheek and walked back to the bed. Dylan did the same. Neither of them took off their shoes, and both were fully clothed.

They just stood there side by side and stared down at the bed.

"This is ridiculous," Collena whispered. "We're adults. We can sleep in the same bed. This is all for Adam."

That was the nudge that Dylan needed, because he climbed into bed. Collena got in, as well. And once again, the silence returned.

"My lawyer is still doing a thorough background check on you," Dylan whispered. "He wants to know if there's anything in your past that Curtis Reese will be able to use against us during the custody fight."

"I've already told you the things he can and will use. My

upbringing, my mother's profession and the undercover assignment that resulted in Adam being stolen."

"What about lovers other than your fiancé? Curtis Reese will use whatever he can," Dylan added when she didn't immediately answer.

It took her several moments to answer. "Other than Sean Reese, I was involved with only one other man. That was... let's see, when I was twenty."

"That's it?" he asked.

"That's it."

He shook his head and gave a lopsided smile of irony. "We're some pair, aren't we? I gave up on love when it became deadly. You apparently gave up on it before you even got started."

Collena mumbled an agreement and wished that she didn't feel anything down deep within her. Because it only made her feel closer to Dylan. Despite their starkly different pasts, they had a lot in common.

Including this troubling attraction.

She wondered if she should address it or, better yet, try to dismiss it. If they talked about it, it might make things worse.

She looked at him again. He hadn't covered up so she still had an incredible view of him. Her eyes went in the wrong direction, traveling the entire length of his body. She even paused in the zipper region, the last place she should be looking. And when she forced her gaze to stop traveling and looked up at Dylan again, she realized he was watching her gawk at him.

Collena waited for embarrassment to flush her cheeks, but it didn't come. She wanted it to come. Because if not, she would look brazen.

She certainly felt brazen.

Worse, Dylan looked it, too. That wasn't a back-off vibe passing between them.

"To hell with this," Dylan grumbled a split second before he slid his hand around the back of her neck and dragged her to him.

It happened so fast that his mouth was on her before Collena realized what was happening. Even then, she had a stupid reaction. Instead of planting her hands on his chest and pushing him away, she heard herself moan a hungry sound of pleasure, and she slung her arms around his neck.

Oh, mercy. He looked good, but he tasted even better. And it'd been a long, long time since she'd kissed a man who knew exactly what he was doing.

The kiss quickly turned hotter. Of course, it'd started out so hot that she was amazed it could get better. Still, she didn't stop it. She deepened it, letting their tongues mate, letting him nip her bottom lip with his teeth.

There was a sharp rap at the door. That was the only warning they got before it opened. They untangled themselves from each other, but not before their visitors saw what was going on. It was Ruth, and Hank was directly behind her.

With everything going on, they'd obviously forgotten to lock the door.

"Oh." Ruth's hand flew to her mouth.

Collena didn't even try to offer an explanation. It would be useless, because she figured she looked well kissed. There was no way to disguise that.

"Is there a problem?" Dylan asked.

Hank nodded. "Millie's not feeling good—she's got

one of her migraines. Ruth and I are going to drive her to the emergency room."

Dylan got up from the bed. "Is there anything I can do to help?"

"No. We'll leave just as soon as Millie's dressed." But Hank didn't move. He stood there and scratched his head. "I was in your office checking on those private detectives, and I saw the report about the fingerprints."

Collena froze, and that question cooled the rest of her passion. "What fingerprints?"

"The ones from the newspaper that you say you found outside your door," Ruth provided. She glared at Dylan. "You didn't trust me when I told you I had nothing to do with putting it there."

"I simply wanted to know whose fingerprints were on it." He turned to Collena. "In addition to a lot of smudges, there were prints from Hank, Millie and Ruth."

"Because we all read that article of lies when it was published five years ago," Hank insisted.

Dylan conceded that with a nod. "I also wanted to check and see if Jonah's prints were there."

"Jonah?" Ruth's hand went to her mouth again. "You think he's doing something to scare off Collena?"

"I don't know. But if so, the newspaper won't help prove that because his prints weren't on it."

"Jonah could have worn gloves," Hank suggested.

Collena silently agreed. In fact, as a police officer, Jonah would have taken steps to cover his tracks.

"What about security surveillance cameras?" Collena asked, wishing she'd thought of it before. She certainly wasn't putting her cop's training to good use.

Dylan shook his head. "That night, I didn't have cameras in the corridors. They only went in today. I'm having the security company install them in all the halls and the common areas."

"If Jonah's behind this," Ruth speculated, "then the cameras probably won't help because he's probably already heard about them. Besides, I doubt he'll be planting any more newspapers."

"What's this about Jonah?" Millie asked. She was squinting, apparently in severe pain.

Millie's posture, however, didn't stop her from looking at Dylan and then Collena. Like her mother and grandfather, Millie probably knew that she and Dylan had just kissed.

"Let's go," Ruth said, gripping her daughter's arm.

Even when the women walked away, Hank still didn't move. "I know I'm not one to give advice," Hank whispered, "but you two should stay away from each other. And you should watch your backs. It's a small town, and it doesn't take long for news to travel. Especially bad news."

"Are you trying to tell me something I don't already know, Hank?" Dylan asked.

"I'm trying to save your *bride's* life. You should get her out of here, Dylan. Send her far away. If not, you're going to have another death on your hands."

DYLAN SAT in his office and stared at the paperwork he needed to be doing. But instead of business, he was thinking about Collena.

They'd shared a restless night in the nursery. Restless, because of the kiss they'd shared. And because of their intense attraction. Hank's warning hadn't helped, either.

Unfortunately, it wouldn't necessarily be safer anywhere else for Collena and Adam. At least with them at the ranch Dylan could personally keep an eye on them. Besides, he and Collena needed to be physically together under the same roof, living as a family, so that it'd help them keep custody.

He checked the security monitor on his desk. It was a split screen that featured the north pasture, the front porch and the playroom where Adam, Collena and Ruth were.

Collena was wearing jeans and a loose red top. While Adam was playing with a toy horse, she stood and went to the window. She was no doubt checking to make sure all was well.

Even on the monitor, he could see that Collena was tired. And beautiful. He couldn't stop his brain from registering that part about her beauty, and it was futile to try. That reckless kiss had sealed his fate. He wanted to kiss her again. He wanted to hold her.

Dylan wanted her in his bed.

Regrettably, she felt the same. Every inch of him was aware of that. Which brought him to the next matter that wouldn't leave his mind. How the hell were they going to keep their hands off each other?

His phone buzzed, and because he needed a change of thought, Dylan quickly glanced at the caller ID. The caller's identity and number were blocked. Dylan answered it anyway.

"Greer," the caller snarled. "It's Curtis Reese."

Dylan instantly went on the defensive. "What do you want?"

"You mean, other than my grandson? I want your butt in jail for making that threatening phone call to my hotel room. That's harassment, Greer."

"That's paranoia, because I didn't call you."

"I don't believe you. And I don't believe this ridiculous pretense of marriage that you have with Collena."

"You know about that?" Dylan was surprised, though he shouldn't be. He knew that, eventually, Curtis would find out.

"Of course, I know. It's all over town. At lunch, that's all the waitress at the diner could talk about. Love at first sight, she said. That's what people in town believe. But you and I know better, don't we? There's no love in that charade of a marriage."

Dylan groaned. *Love at first sight.* That was not what he wanted people in Greer to be discussing. "You probably set the waitress straight, huh?"

"I didn't say a word to her. If the town wants to believe you married Collena for love, then let them. A judge will see it for what it is—a desperate attempt by two desperate people who aren't fit to raise a child."

Dylan detected some movement in the doorway, and he looked up and spotted Collena. That top and jeans looked even better in person.

It's Curtis Reese, Dylan mouthed.

She rolled her eyes and sighed.

"Unless you plan to drop this custody suit," Dylan told the man, "then any future calls should go through my lawyer. If not, I'll consider them harassment."

Dylan hung up, but he knew it wasn't the last he'd hear from Curtis.

"He's going to do everything he can to make our lives miserable," Collena said. She walked closer and looked down at him. "Ruth said a friend of a friend called to say that everyone in town is talking about us."

So, there it was—confirmed gossip. Curtis hadn't been just blowing smoke. "I heard."

She made a sound deep in her throat and stood there, almost stoically, but Dylan knew this information was causing a firestorm inside her.

"Maybe the person who killed your sister and fiancée is long gone." Her voice was a little unsteady, and she sank down onto the edge of his desk.

Because she looked as weary as he felt, Dylan stood and pulled her into his arms. Yes, it was stupid. Reckless, even. But it didn't seem to matter. To the town of Greer, they were a couple, and that news would likely get back to a killer.

If there was a killer.

Maybe, just maybe, fate would decide that both of them had already been through enough, and the person responsible for the deaths was either already locked away for other crimes or else dead. Dylan didn't care which; he just wanted the person away from Collena and Adam.

"You want a drink to steady your nerves?" he asked.

She shook her head. "I don't drink. I have a low tolerance for alcohol." She pulled back and met his gaze. "Besides, with so much going on, I should keep a clear head."

"I agree."

But he kissed her anyway.

It was worse than the kiss the night before because this one came naturally. It was as if he'd kissed her a thousand times. Too bad that feeling didn't satiate the fire growing inside him.

He stopped, ran his tongue over his lips and was pleased to taste her there.

"I'll bet you're going to remind me that kissing you is a mistake," he said.

She shook her head. "No, but I should remind myself." Collena reached out and smoothed her hand over his face. "Maybe we knew each other in a past life or something. Maybe that's why we feel so connected."

Surprised and amused, he flexed his eyebrows. "You believe in past lives?"

"Not really. But I've gone through all the logical answers and have moved on to the illogical ones to explain why I'm so attracted to you. I want to have sex with you." She wagged her index finger at him to stop him from jumping on that. "It wasn't an invitation."

Dylan knew that. She was fighting this as much as he was. And, like him, she was failing. Still, it was easier to think of the attraction than the other realities that were nipping at their heels.

"We could just try it," he offered, tongue-in-cheek. "Maybe we'd suck in bed together."

"Suck," she repeated, flexing her eyebrows. "You know it wouldn't suck. It would probably be the best experience I've ever had, and it would do all sorts of things to remind me that I'm a woman."

"You don't like to be reminded of that?" he asked, serious now.

"Let's just say that, as a woman, I've made choices that weren't always good. So, I'm trying to think more like a mother and more like a cop."

"Cops and mothers can still have sex."

She frowned at his smile and used her fingers to draw down the corners of his mouth. The heat rifled through his body. And he instantly wanted more. With her touching his face. With them so close that all he had to do was reach out, pull her to him and kiss her again.

But Collena put an end to that short fantasy. She moved away from him and went to the French doors that led to the side yard and pasture. Her maneuver didn't mean this discussion was over. Far from it. The attraction wasn't going away and, sooner or later, they'd have to address it.

"Adam is amazing," Collena said with her back to him. "When he wakes up from his afternoon nap, I thought maybe the three of us could do something together."

"I'd like that." In fact, that felt as inviting as the whole idea of having sex with Collena.

And that meant he was in serious trouble here.

Collena glanced at him over her shoulder. There was a hint of a smile on her face.

The moment seemed to freeze.

Dylan sensed that something was wrong a split second too late.

A bullet crashed through the glass panes of the French doors.

Chapter Ten

The sound of the shot registered in Collena's head just as Dylan and she drove to the floor.

It was just in time, because the next bullet shattered the glass right in front of where she'd been standing.

The adrenaline was quick, hitting her hard and causing her blood pressure and heart rate to spike. She didn't have her gun. She'd left it in her room when she went to spend time with Adam.

That could turn out to be a fatal mistake.

Because someone wanted them dead. Rodney Harmon, probably. He'd found her, and this time, he'd come to deliver on that promise to kill her.

Dylan scrambled to the side and took her with him. He also put himself in between those bullets and her body. It was admirable. Heroic, even. But she wanted to throttle him for nearly getting himself killed to save her.

"My gun's in the desk drawer," he said. His breath was rough.

Collena knew what that meant—the desk drawer was in the line of fire. Whoever was shooting at them would be able to hit Dylan or her if they went after the gun.

The same was true is they tried to get to the door that led to the corridor.

They were trapped.

There was another shot. Then another. Both tore through the thick glass and sent it spewing across the room. Collena ducked down and sheltered her eyes to prevent being hit.

"Where's your phone?" she asked.

He shook his head. "On the desk."

Both of them cursed. Someone had to get to the phone. They had to warn Ruth to keep Adam safe and they had to call the sheriff. Of course, someone in the house had likely heard the shots by now. After all, the two P.I.s were in a guest room that they'd converted to an office. Maybe the sheriff was already on the way.

Or Jonah, if the sheriff had sent him again instead.

And that caused Collena's heart rate to spike even more. If Rodney Harmon was indeed out there shooting at them, she didn't think Jonah would do much to deter him.

Two more bullets slammed through the door, each of them taking huge bites out of the wood. Splinters and glass pelted them.

"The gunman's closer," Dylan said.

Collena lifted her head and listened. The next shot confirmed that.

The gunman was moving toward the house. Toward their son.

Oh, God.

The shooter was armed with a high-powered rifle and might start firing into the nursery where Adam was napping.

"I have to get my gun and phone," Dylan informed her. He started to move, but she latched on to his arm.

"It'd be suicide. We need some kind of diversion."

Collena glanced around the room, looking for something—anything—while the gunman continued to blast through the French doors. They didn't have much time. The shots were getting closer, and there wouldn't be much of the doors left as a barrier once the gunman made it to them.

"Throw anything you can get your hands on at the French doors," Dylan ordered.

Collena considered his plan. It wasn't much of a diversion, but it was the only one they had. She prayed it would work, and she grabbed the pillows from the cozy chairs next to the fireplace.

"Now," Dylan said.

She hurled the first pillow at the door and quickly followed it with another. Collena didn't stop there. She stood and grabbed the items from the mantel. Pictures, flowers and even a heavy brass horse figurine all flew in the direction of the doors. Hopefully, she was creating a visual barrier for Dylan.

But the gunman didn't stop.

At a furious, almost frantic pace, the bullets began to rip through the house.

Dylan sprang into action. With the objects flying through the air, he dove toward his desk, landing amid the glass, splinters and debris.

Collena pushed her concern and fear for him aside and started to throw the books from the side shelves that flanked the fireplace. When she saw Dylan reach up, she knew he was at the most vulnerable point of this plan to retrieve his gun and phone. She had to do something more.

But what?

Out of the corner of her eye, she saw Dylan make his move to the desk. Collena looked up and spotted the painting over the fireplace. It was the only thing within her reach that was large enough to do any good. She ripped it from the wall, and while Dylan lifted his head to grab what he needed, she stuck out the painting and tried to use it as a barrier.

A shot tore through the canvas.

"Hurry!" she shouted to Dylan.

There wasn't much left of the glass, but there was enough wood in the door frame to pose a significant risk to both of them. But it wasn't nearly as big a risk as not getting the phone and his gun. They needed the items to keep Adam safe.

Dylan grabbed both from the desk and dove back toward the fireplace. Collena dropped the shredded picture and took his cell phone. Dylan rattled off the number to her so she could call the line in the nursery and playroom. A line that Ruth should have answered.

She didn't.

That did it. Collena went from being afraid to being terrified. Her son had to be all right.

She tried the number again, while the bullets continued to riddle the house. Dylan called out a new set of numbers, and Collena frantically pressed them in.

Ina, the cook, finally answered.

"What's going on? What's that noise?" the woman shouted. "Is somebody shootin' at us?"

"Yes. Stay down and try to let Ruth know what's happening so she can keep Adam away from the windows."

"I will. I already called Sheriff Hathaway and told him to get himself out here."

Thank God. But Collena immediately rethought that. "Is he bringing Jonah?"

"No. He said Jonah wasn't there so he said he'd come himself. He called in the night-shift deputy who's supposed to meet him here."

That was good. *If* they made it in time.

"Try to check on Adam," Collena instructed. "And let the two P.I.s know what's going on. Just don't come into Dylan's office. Don't even get near the door. Because that's where Dylan and I are pinned down, and it's where the gunman is shooting."

Collena ended the call so she could keep the line open in case the sheriff tried to phone them.

Dylan inched toward the gaping holes in the French doors, took a quick look and then pulled back.

"I don't see anyone," he relayed to her.

That meant the gunman was likely using the outbuildings as cover. But it didn't explain how the person had gotten there in the first place. The security monitors should have detected the movement. Or the P.I.s should have spotted someone skulking across the property. Did that mean the system had malfunctioned?

Or had someone tampered with it?

There was a lull in the shooting, and Dylan levered himself up to get a better look. Collena saw him stiffen, and he took aim.

He fired.

So did the shooter.

The bullet came so close to him that Collena could practically feel it. It slammed into the far wall near the corridor door.

Dylan started to fire again, but Collena pulled him back.

It was a good thing, too, because the next barrage of bullets pelted the room, hitting everything in their path.

Collena scrambled to the corner, using the thick stone fireplace as cover—the bullets couldn't penetrate that. She also kept a firm grip on Dylan's arm and tried to prevent him from attempting to return fire. While she wanted him to do that for Adam's sake, she knew it was simply too big a risk to take. She had to hold on to the hope that the nursery was out of the gunman's reach.

They had to make sure it stayed that way.

"The sheriff will be here soon," she reminded him. And herself. She silently repeated it like a mantra.

Her heartbeat was so loud in her ears that it took her a moment to realize she was hearing the sound of a siren. Hopefully, from the sheriff's squad car.

Dylan looked at her. His eyes were wide and vigilant. And then he cursed.

Because the shots stopped.

"The gunman's getting away," Dylan insisted. He tried to rear up, but again Collena restrained him.

"You can't go out there," she warned. "It could be an ambush."

"He could be going after Adam."

That realization was like a knife to her heart.

With their gazes locked, she released the grip she had on him and got to her feet, as well. "Not outside," she whispered. "We can go through the corridors and get to the nursery."

Of course, that didn't mean the gunman wasn't waiting for them to do just that. The person could have a rifle aimed at the one spot that they would try to get to: the corridor door.

"We can dive behind the desk and use it as cover," Dylan suggested. But he didn't just suggest it. He dove, landing behind the thick oak that would hopefully shield him from any more bullets.

Collena was about to start her own dive when she heard the sound.

A sound that stopped her heart—breaking glass.

And it came from the other side of the house.

"ADAM," DYLAN WHISPERED. He had to get to his son. Because that sound could mean the gunman was breaking into the nursery.

"Go!" Collena shouted to him.

Dylan did. He didn't wait for Collena, and prayed she could stay out of the line of fire. Instead, he crawled to the door, opened it and scurried into the corridor. Once there, he got to his feet and started racing toward the nursery.

He checked over his shoulder and saw that Collena wasn't too far behind him. She wasn't armed, and he couldn't take the time to find her a weapon. Every second was crucial.

There was another crash. Not a bullet. More broken glass. It'd probably come from a window where someone was trying to break in.

Dylan ran faster, and it seemed as if the siren from the sheriff's car got louder with each running step he took. He didn't even pause when he got to the nursery. Dylan threw open the door.

Adam was sleeping in his crib. There was no broken glass anywhere.

Behind him, he heard his cell phone ring, and Collena answered it as she ducked into the nursery with him.

"It's the sheriff," she relayed to him. "He spotted some-one running away from the house, and he's going in pursuit."

Well, that was a start, but it wouldn't do squat for them if the gunman backtracked. "Lock the door," he told Col-lena. "Move the crib away from the windows and to the corner of the room."

She immediately began to do as he asked. "Where's Ruth?"

"I don't know." But he intended to find out. For now, he took up watch by one of the trio of floor-to-ceiling win-dows in the nursery.

Once Collena had moved the crib, she grabbed the se-curity monitor from the changing table and began to flip through the various camera angles.

"Do you see anything?" Dylan asked. Because from the window, he didn't see either the sheriff or the shooter.

"The entire screen is nothing but static."

Dylan cursed again. He didn't think that was a coinci-dence. And while he was thinking, he tried to put a name to the person who'd just tried to kill them.

Rodney Harmon, probably.

But he wasn't about to rule out anyone just yet. "Call Ina," Dylan instructed. "Find out where everyone is and if they're safe."

He watched, waiting, as Collena made the call. She kept her voice low, practically at a whisper, so she wouldn't wake Adam.

"Ina's okay," she said several moments later. "But she's alone in the kitchen. She doesn't know where anyone else is."

That was not what Dylan wanted to hear. Even if Ruth,

Millie and Hank were nowhere to be found, at least the two P.I.s should have heard something from the guest suite where they'd set up their office. But thankfully, he heard something that he welcomed. Sheriff Hathaway's voice.

"Dylan, it's me—don't shoot."

Dylan opened the window as the sheriff approached the exterior of the house. "Please tell me you got the gunman."

The lanky, sandy-haired sheriff still had his gun drawn, and he was still darting glances all around him. He shook his head. "Afraid not. I didn't even get a good look at him. The person was dressed all in black and was wearing a ski mask."

Hell. "Could it have been Rodney Harmon?"

"Coulda been anybody." He tipped his head toward the back porch. "I'm coming in through the kitchen. Stay put until I've had a chance to look around."

Dylan welcomed the help because he didn't want to leave Adam and Collena until he was sure that it was safe.

He kept guard at the window and listened for any sound to indicate that an intruder was in the house.

And then he saw Ruth.

The woman was coming out of one of the barns. She was dressed in her pants and a sweater top, but she wasn't wearing a coat. Maybe she'd heard the gunfire and hidden there. But if so, why hadn't she tried to get to Adam? That should have been her first priority, even above her own safety.

"If Rodney Harmon is behind this, he won't stop," he heard Collena say.

Dylan glanced back at her. She was standing guard over the crib, but she was also looking out one of the other windows. She'd seen Ruth, as well.

"*If* he's behind this," Dylan clarified. But he couldn't be positive that he was.

Too many things had gone wrong since Collena's arrival, and while it was true that Harmon wanted to kill her, Dylan couldn't rule out that someone else might have been responsible for this shooting.

"It's me—Sheriff Hathaway," said a voice from the other side of the door.

With his gun still ready, Dylan went to the door and opened it.

"No sign of a gunman inside," the sheriff volunteered. "But someone not only shot out the doors in your office, they shot the windows in the dining room. And those two guys in that room at the end of the hall have been drugged or something. They're knocked out cold, and there's an empty pizza box sitting on the coffee table."

The pizza they'd had delivered just an hour earlier.

"Ina says there's something wonky with your security system," the sheriff continued. His attention went to Collena. "Here's what I think happened. About two minutes before I got Ina's call about the shooting here, I got a call from Marla Jenkins's boy. He was supposed to be delivering pizza out here, but he says someone sneaked up behind him and hit him with something. A shovel, he thinks. Next thing he knew he was tied up and shut in the Dumpster outside the pizza place."

"You think the man who delivered the pizza was Rodney Harmon?" Collena asked. Adam stirred, and Collena tried to soothe him by rubbing his back. Dylan wished he could do something to soothe her because Collena was pale again, and her hands were trembling.

"I think that's a strong possibility."

Dylan processed that, and he didn't come to a good conclusion. "If it was Harmon, then why didn't he just shoot his way in when the P.I.s opened the door? Why would he sneak onto the property posing as a delivery man, only to then walk at least two hundred yards away before he started shooting?"

The sheriff lifted his shoulder. "I don't have an answer for that." He studied Dylan. "But I'm guessing you might have some idea?"

He did, but he didn't have time to voice it before he heard footsteps. The sheriff turned, but immediately relaxed. "It's Ruth."

Collena moved protectively in front of Adam.

"Is the trouble over?" Ruth asked. She peered past the sheriff and looked at Dylan.

"Where were you?" Dylan asked, and he was certain it sounded just the way he meant it—as an accusation.

Ruth drew back her shoulders. "Outside, checking on that new mare. I stayed there and hid when I heard the shots. Why?"

"Are you willing to let the sheriff test you for gunshot residue?"

Her mouth dropped open. "What are you saying, Dylan? Do you think I'm responsible for what happened?"

He shook his head. "I don't know, but I know I can't risk having you here."

"What's going on, Mother?" Millie asked from the corridor. Several moments later, she joined Ruth and stood side by side with her. Both of them stared accusingly at Dylan.

Ruth didn't answer her daughter, but Dylan did. "I think it's best if you, Ruth and Hank move to the hotel in town for a while. Until we can get all of this straightened out."

"What's to straighten out?" Ruth asked. She fired a nasty glance at Collena. "You're responsible for this. You've been trying to come between Dylan and me since you stepped foot in this house."

"I only want to make sure Adam is safe," Collena answered.

"No. You don't want to share Dylan or Adam with anyone. Especially with me." With each word, the anger in her voice climbed, and Dylan could see a vein bulging on her neck. "I raised Dylan. He's as much a son to me as if I'd given birth to him. That doesn't mean I can't see when he's making a mistake."

"Let's go, Mother," Millie said, taking Ruth's arm.

But Ruth held her ground and glared at Collena. Dylan stepped between them so he could make eye contact with Ruth. "This isn't Collena's fault. I'm the one who wants you to move out."

"I'll never believe that. She's just like your sister—can't you see that? Demanding. Manipulating. Always trying to have you to herself."

Dylan felt himself freeze. "What did you say?"

Ruth stilled, and she frantically shook her head. "Nothing."

Millie tried to pull Ruth out of the room, but Dylan stopped both women. However, he directed his question to Ruth. "Do you know something about my sister's death?"

"She knows nothing," Hank said. He was in the corridor, just behind the sheriff. "And this conversation is over."

Hank brushed past the sheriff and grabbed both women by their arms.

Millie looked back at Dylan. "I need to tell you something."

"Talking time is over," Hank declared. And he hurried Millie out the door before she could say anything else.

Chapter Eleven

Collena glanced around her suite and made sure everything was checked off her mental list. They'd decided to stay in her suite rather than Dylan's because there were fewer windows and because his had French doors that led to an outside patio.

The crib was in place—tucked in the corner of the bedroom away from any windows and doors. Since it was already close to midnight, Adam was sound asleep, resting beneath a pale blue blanket, with his favorite stuffed horse snuggled against his chest.

All the windows were locked and the curtains drawn. Collena had checked that; so had Dylan and the two P.I.s. The security system was set for the interior and the perimeter of the ranch. Both she and Dylan were armed, and one of the P.I.s was standing guard outside the suite door to make sure no one got in. The other was in the family room on the other side of the house and would keep watch on the motion-activated security monitor.

In other words, they'd done everything they could to keep Adam and themselves out of harm's way.

It had to be enough.

Because Collena didn't even want to consider the alternative. She couldn't go through another round of shooting. It'd taken ten years off her life when she'd realized that Adam could have been hurt.

However, the shots all seemed to be aimed at Dylan and her. Or maybe the bullets had been meant solely for her and the shooter had been willing to take Dylan out during the process. Either way, it could have been a deadly situation, and they were lucky to be alive.

Collena had taken a long shower once Adam had fallen asleep around eight o'clock. The steamy hot water had helped relax her a little. So had the herbal tea and turkey sandwich that Ina had fixed for her. But Collena wasn't holding out hope that she would get much sleep tonight. She'd be listening for any sound or sign that the gunman had returned for another round.

Dylan was pacing in the sitting room while he talked to the sheriff. It was his sixth call to the man since the shooting. Collena figured there'd be many more but hopefully not tonight. Dylan was exhausted, and it was obvious that nothing was going to be accomplished at this late hour.

"No sign of Rodney Harmon," Dylan said in a whisper to her when he ended the call.

It'd been too much to hope differently. Besides, the security system was fixed now. Or rather, it was now turned on. Shortly before the shooting, someone had apparently disarmed it using the power-supply box located outside the house. Or maybe it had just malfunctioned on its own. Just in case, Dylan had given the box a new lock and had made it tamperproof.

She hoped.

Collena walked toward him. A closer look revealed his

sleep-weary eyes and the way stress had tightened the muscles in his face. "What do you think Millie wanted to say before Hank forced her to leave?"

He rubbed his forehead. "I don't know—maybe that her mother is a killer. Ruth certainly let something slip with that comment about my sister."

Yes. Collena had gone over that a hundred times. "It could mean nothing."

"It could mean everything," Dylan countered. He sank down on the foot of the bed. "I'm going to contact their therapist, but it's hard for me to accept that, for all these years, I might have had a killer living beneath my roof."

"I know." Because he looked as if he could use it, she touched his arm and rubbed it gently. "But Rodney Harmon is still our number-one suspect. When he's caught, then you can decide if you want to smooth things over with Ruth and the others. In the meantime, you need to get some rest."

He turned toward her. "You know I'm not leaving this room, right?"

"I know." She didn't want him to leave. As difficult as it would be for them to spend another night together, Collena wanted Dylan close in case something went wrong.

He reached out, hooked his arm around her and pulled her onto the bed with him. Apparently, he didn't have anything sexual in mind because he simply maneuvered them to the head of the bed so their heads were on the pillows, and then he pulled the side of the comforter over them.

Collena was still dressed in jeans and a loose shirt, but she was also wearing her shoulder holster and weapon. It was digging into her side, so she sat up, slipped it off and put it on the nightstand. In the process of removing the holster, one side of her top slipped off her shoulder. She quickly tried to put it back in place.

But Dylan noticed the scar.

"What happened there?" He traced the still-pink scar with his finger.

"Gunshot wound." She wanted to keep the explanation short, but Dylan questioned her with his stare. "One of the investors at the Brighton Birthing Center was aiming at someone else—another victim—but shot me instead. Don't worry. He's in a maximum-security prison. In addition to shooting me, he was responsible for the death of another woman."

"Did he have any part in what happened to you right after Adam was born?" he asked after a long pause.

"Probably not." She carefully put her gun on the nightstand close enough that she could still reach it. "I think that was all Rodney Harmon."

Anger went through his eyes. "It makes me sick to think that he was even in the same room with you and Adam, and at a time when you were so vulnerable. You'd just given birth, for God's sake, and he used you like a punching bag."

She heard the sympathy in his voice and could see it in his expression. It had been there since he'd seen that photo taken of her shortly after the attack.

"I know what's going on," she said at the end of a heavy sigh. "You're not really attracted to me. You have this male need to safeguard me. You're a natural protector."

He continued to stare at her. "I wasn't able to protect Julie and Abigail."

"Not from lack of trying." She considered giving Dylan a reassuring hug. But even reassuring hugs could get out of hand. "The need to protect me is now all mixed up with what you think is attraction."

"What I think is attraction," he repeated. There was a dangerous edge to his voice, as if she'd just pushed a button that shouldn't have been pushed.

The air between them changed.

He changed.

That edge slipped into his eyes.

Collena didn't back away. She wasn't afraid of him. But she was afraid of what she'd started. So much for analyzing him and blowing off the attraction.

"Let's test your theory," he said. "Let's see if there's any lust buried beneath all that need to protect you."

And with that, he reached out lightning fast.

He latched on to a handful of her hair and pulled her to him. Before Collena could even catch her breath, Dylan lowered his head and took her mouth as if he owned her.

Of course, Dylan hadn't needed the kiss to prove that lust to him, but he wanted to prove it to Collena. Why, he didn't know. And maybe proving it was simply an excuse to do something he'd been wanting to do for hours. Kiss her. Taste her. Hold her. And then push hard and deep into her until she quit trying to dismiss the attraction between them.

But she wasn't dismissing anything.

From the moment his mouth touched hers, Collena became a willing participant. She kissed him right back. She also lifted her arms, first one, then the other. She slid them around his neck, brushing his chest with her breasts.

The contact only made him want more.

So, he took the kisses to her neck. It was a temporary stopping point, but he lingered a while when he realized it was a sensitive area for Collena. Her fingers began to dig into his back and, with gentle pressure from her palms, she urged him closer.

So Dylan got closer. A lot closer.

Pushing her back onto the bed, he shoved up her top and dropped some kisses on the exposed parts of her breasts. Collena made a sound of raw pleasure and arched against him.

It aligned their bodies, her sex against his. And as if that weren't enough, she slid her hand between them and ran her fingers over his erection.

Dylan lost his breath.

He didn't care if he ever found it.

The attraction and lust turned to a full blazing fire. He wanted her, bad, but he also didn't want to skip any of the things that he'd been fantasizing about. And one of those fantasies had been to strip her naked and kiss every inch of her.

Dylan started by unhooking the front clasp of her bra, spilling her breasts out into his hands. Now, it was his turn to moan as he kissed her and tongued her erect nipples. It was pure pleasure.

And pure torture.

Because each taste of her only made Dylan want her even more.

Still, he continued the kisses, pleasing both her and himself, and he made his way from her breasts to her stomach. He unbuttoned her jeans and slid down the zipper so he could sample the silky area around her navel. It was another sensitive spot. As he gently sucked her, she lifted her hips, offering him more of her.

That's when he knew the jeans had to go.

He peeled them off her and was more than happy to find a tiny swatch of white lace. He could see the triangle of blond hair beneath. And that lace was the only thing standing between him and Collena's sex.

Because he couldn't wait, he tasted her through the lace. That earned him some unspoken praise as Collena wound her fingers into his hair and slipped her legs over his back.

Dylan figured they were on the brink of something incredible.

He figured wrong.

Because that's when it hit him that something was missing.

He lifted his head and cursed. "No condom."

"No condom," she repeated in a whisper. And she repeated it again through her heavy gusts of breath.

"There are some in my bedroom." He got up, fully intending to leave.

But Collena stopped him. "The P.I. is outside the door."

"So?"

"So, you can't go out there with that." She ran her bare foot over the front of his jeans and damn near made him climax in the process.

"Trust me, I can go out there like this." It wouldn't be comfortable, and it'd be a little embarrassing, but at least he and Collena would get to have sex.

Unfortunately, going out there would mean leaving Collena and Adam.

And that wasn't a smart idea.

His body begged to differ, but Dylan offered his body an alternative.

"There's more than one way to go about this," he suggested to Collena. After all, he'd already started in that direction.

"No." She shook her head and tugged her jeans back up. She also redid her bra and lowered her top over her breasts. "We shouldn't even be doing this."

He knew she was right, but he wasn't ready to give up just yet. "Please remind me why."

"Adam might wake up. Also someone is after us. We need to stay focused. Somehow, I don't think we can stay focused if your mouth is…occupied."

She was right again.

Damn her.

"I should have stopped before we got started," she grumbled. "But you got me hot. And I can't think straight when you kiss me."

Dylan was still aching. Well, throbbing actually. But it made him feel marginally better that he'd made her a little crazy. "You're admitting that?"

She nodded. Then, she huffed. "I can't deny the attraction I have for you. Or the way you make me feel. I also can't deny that we'll act on that attraction. Because we probably will. But I have to wonder where sex will lead us. Once the passion is all burned out, we still need to be friends so we can raise Adam together."

He frowned. There was an argument in her logic, and Dylan would have started it, too, if there hadn't been a knock at the door.

Just like that, his heart went into overdrive. He prepared himself for the worst. So did she. Collena grabbed her gun, and Dylan barreled out of the bed to go to the suite door.

"What's wrong?" Dylan asked the P.I. without opening the door.

"The deputy sheriff is here to see you."

Dylan checked his watch. It was nearly twelve-thirty in the morning. "At this hour?"

"He says it's important."

It'd better be. "Wait here with Adam and Collena," Dylan instructed the P.I. Dylan wanted her far away from the deputy, just in case Jonah was a killer and this was some kind of ambush.

With his gun in hand and an angry expression on his face, Dylan stormed toward the front door. He found the other P.I. and Jonah waiting in the foyer. Jonah didn't have his gun drawn, but he had a perturbed expression that, no doubt, matched Dylan's.

"What's this about?" Dylan demanded.

"Business," Jonah snarled back. "There's been a murder, and I need to know if you're the one who committed it."

Chapter Twelve

Collena glanced at the clock.

And paced.

Dylan had been gone over ten minutes. Not a lifetime, but considering the potential danger that was all around them, it felt like forever to her.

She checked Adam, who was still sleeping. Then Collena opened the door just a fraction to make sure the P.I. was still there. He was.

"Do you know what the deputy wanted with Dylan?" she asked the P.I.

He shook his head.

And that's when Collena knew she'd waited long enough. Deputy Jonah Burke was their suspect, and by now he could have done all sorts of things to Dylan and the other P.I. She grabbed her gun and the baby monitor so she could keep an eye on Adam. She also ordered the P.I. to stay put and guard the baby while she went in search of Dylan.

Collena listened as she hurried down the corridor. There were no shouts, no sounds of violence. Nor was there any indication that Dylan was under attack. And she confirmed that once she made it to the foyer. Dylan was leaning against the wall, and he was staring at Jonah, who was only a few feet away from him.

"What's wrong?" Collena immediately asked. She knew something had happened from their bleak expressions.

"Curtis Reese is dead," Jonah announced. "Someone murdered him."

Her breath clogged in her throat, and though she had a dozen questions about whom, when and how, she couldn't ask any of them. She could only stand there and try to absorb what she'd just heard.

Curtis Reese was dead.

She hated that she felt even marginal relief over the custody issue. But Collena couldn't feel any happiness that a man had been murdered. After all, Curtis might have been a pigheaded snob, but he wasn't a criminal, and he didn't deserve to die.

"A hunter found Reese's body not far from here," Jonah continued. "Only about an eighth of a mile from where your car was burned."

Collena wondered if that was a coincidence. Had Curtis been there when he was killed, or had the killer deposited the body there as some kind of warning to them?

She walked to Dylan and touched his arm. The gesture brought his gaze to hers. Dylan was obviously as upset and shocked about this as she was.

"I was just telling Dylan," Jonah went on, "that it's hard to tell much of anything because Reese's body was badly burned. But it looks like he was shot first and then set on fire."

"He was burned?" Collena asked, though she had to say it twice for the words to have any sounds.

Jonah nodded. "Similarly to the way Abigail and Julie

were killed. Except their accidents were caused by electrical fires. Reese's car had been doused with gasoline that someone siphoned from the tank."

Jonah didn't add anything else. He just stared at them, and she soon realized why he was really at the house.

"Neither Dylan, nor I killed Curtis Reese," Collena volunteered.

"So Dylan already said. He also said you were both here at the house all day and night. Is that true?"

"Yes. With Rodney Harmon on the loose, it wouldn't have been safe for us to go out." She paused. "How long has Curtis been dead?"

"Don't know yet. The coroner might be able to pinpoint the time of death, but with the burns, that might not be so easy."

"But you're sure it's Curtis?" she clarified.

Jonah nodded. "The sheriff got the name of Curtis's dentist from his housekeeper, and we e-mailed him some pictures of his teeth. The dentist made a preliminary match. Plus, the housekeeper was able to ID his shoes and watch."

That wasn't one-hundred-percent proof, but on the other hand, she knew of no reason Curtis or anyone else would fake his death.

"We're the only suspects," Dylan told her.

"Then, you'd better find other possibilities," Collena insisted, talking to Jonah. "Because if you're sure this was murder—"

"We're sure. And as for those other possibilities, perhaps you can suggest some."

"Rodney Harmon," she said without hesitation. "He's out there somewhere, and he's a killer. Maybe Curtis had the misfortune to cross paths with him. After all, they're both in Greer."

"And what motive would Harmon have to kill a perfect stranger?" Jonah didn't wait for them to answer. "Because as far as I can tell, Curtis Reese didn't have any connection to the Brighton Birthing Center or to Rodney Harmon."

Collena opened her mouth, closed it and glanced at Dylan. Was he thinking what she was thinking? That maybe Ruth, Hank or Millie had done this?

Unfortunately, they had motives.

And that motive was Adam.

Collena wasn't sure she could trust the three of them, but she had no doubts about their love for Adam. Could one of them have eliminated Curtis because he was a threat to Dylan's claim to custody?

Mercy.

Was one of them a killer after all?

Dylan didn't offer any speculation about his former nanny and the members of her family. Nor did Collena. It was best for her to do some digging before she pointed a finger at anyone.

"Once the coroner's done with the autopsy," Jonah continued, "I want you both to come to the police station for questioning." He shifted his stance and eyed Collena. "Because the way I see it, there were only two people who had a reason to kill Curtis Reese, and those two people are you and Dylan."

WHILE DYLAN WAITED on hold for a report from his lead P.I., he continued to review the surveillance videos taken around the perimeter of the ranch.

He'd set up a makeshift office in his bedroom. It wasn't well equipped since the shooting, but he'd managed to salvage his desk and most of his computer equipment. Thankfully the security disks had been spared by the bullets so he was able to view the section of the ranch near the fence where they'd found Curtis Reese's body.

Dylan saw the flames in the distance. But not the killer. The darkness had concealed his identity, giving them nothing new.

Now, on top of everything else, Collena and he were murder suspects. Not just in Jonah's eyes, either. The brief conversation that Dylan had had that morning with Sheriff Hathaway was more than enough for Dylan to realize that since he and Collena had a motive, the authorities weren't interested in looking elsewhere.

Dylan was.

That's why he hadn't refused Millie's request when she phoned and said she wanted to come out to the ranch to talk to Collena and him. He didn't exactly relish the idea of having Millie around right now, but he wanted to question her about Curtis Reese's murder. Dylan only hoped that Millie didn't know anything about it.

He wanted this pinned on Rodney Harmon.

Dylan opened his desk drawer and searched for a mint or some gum. His mouth was parched from the central heating and the fact it'd been a while since he'd bothered to eat or drink anything. When he found nothing in the center drawer, he went through the side ones.

And he found the condoms.

They'd been there for months. He'd bought them at a time when he was certain he was ready to risk having an actual sex life. The bulk of the box was still there. Sad. And it was probably dangerous to think of Collena and condoms and then pair them in the same thought, but he did.

He took one of the foil packs and slipped it into his pocket. Dylan thought of Collena again and grabbed a second one. Yes, there was something calculating about carrying around condoms, but he also wasn't stupid. Sooner or later, they'd land in bed, and this time he was going to be prepared.

Dylan heard the doorbell and knew that one of the P.I.s would screen the visitor. He checked the surveillance monitor and saw Millie standing on the front porch. The P.I. let her in and, as Dylan had instructed him to do, the man led her toward the family room.

"Dylan," the lead P.I., Mason Tanner, said from the other end of the phone line. "Sorry that it took me so long. I was trying to gather reports from all my men. I've got six working on this, including Angelo Cardona and Ron Cowan, the two at your house."

Dylan hoped it was enough. "And has anyone found anything?"

"We're going through the security disks that the bank manager and some of the store owners let us use. No more Rodney Harmon sightings, but using the disks, I was able to verify that Curtis Reese left his hotel room about eight o'clock last night. An eyewitness saw him driving in the direction of your ranch."

That wasn't really news, considering Reese had been found on the property bordering the ranch.

"The sheriff brought in the Rangers to go through the crime scene," Mason continued. "That's good news for us since I was able to get my hands on their preliminary report. Reese had some pretty expensive surveillance gear in his car. Binoculars, video equipment and even a long-range eavesdropping device. He went to those woods to spy on you, Dylan."

And got killed in the process.

"Did the town surveillance disks show anyone leaving shortly after Curtis?" Dylan asked.

"Yeah. It could mean nothing though. Could be a coincidence."

Dylan wasn't sure he believed in coincidences. "Who was it?"

"Your employee, Millie Sayers."

Dylan groaned softly.

"I was going to find Millie and talk to her," Mason explained.

"No need." Dylan glanced at the house surveillance screen again and spotted something he definitely didn't want to see. Millie was in the family room, all right. But she wasn't alone.

Collena was with her.

And it appeared the two were arguing.

"Call me if you find anything else," Dylan said to Mason. He hung up so he could hurry. But once he got close to the family room, he realized the women weren't arguing.

They were discussing him.

He stopped just outside the door and listened.

"So, you're admitting that you're in love with Dylan?" Collena asked.

Millie didn't answer right away. "Yes. I've been in love with him for a long time."

Well, that's the first he'd heard of it. Millie had certainly kept her feelings hidden.

Or had she?

Dylan mentally backtracked and recalled the looks she'd given him. He also recalled how upset she'd been when he announced his engagement five years ago. Still, she'd never said anything about loving him.

"Mother was always trying to push me to get together with Dylan," Millie continued. Her voice sounded heavy, as if she were fighting back tears. "I told her it was useless, that Dylan didn't see me that way, that he thought of me as a sister. But she believed I could change his mind."

Collena made a sound of understanding. "Is it possible that your mother decided to…eliminate Dylan's fiancée so you'd stand a better chance with him?"

Until Collena had asked that, Dylan had been ready to end his eavesdropping and go into the family room, but now he paused a moment longer. Because that was the question he needed answered.

"My mother wanted me to come and talk to you," Millie said. Which obviously wasn't an answer to Collena's question at all. "She said if I didn't come clean with you she'd tell Dylan *today* how I feel about him. And she would. My mother believes if you know that I love him, that you'll back away so that Dylan and I can have a chance at a real relationship."

Collena shook her head. "Dylan and I are together because of Adam. I can't back away. Besides, have you talked to Dylan about this? Because I don't think he'll back away from me, either."

"You're right," Millie said a moment later. "Still, my mother thought I should try. She wants what's best for me, and despite what you think of her, she wouldn't hurt anyone. Neither would my grandfather." She paused. "At least I hope they wouldn't."

Oh, man.

That was Dylan's cue to make himself known, and he had every intention of pressing Millie to explain why she had doubts about her own flesh and blood.

"Dylan," Millie said the moment she detected his presence in the room. "Thank you for letting me come."

"I hope you came with answers." Dylan crossed the room so he could stand beside Collena.

"Maybe." Millie suddenly looked very uncomfortable. She glanced at Collena as if she might ask her to leave, but she didn't. Instead, Millie reached in her coat pocket and took out something.

Dylan reached for his gun in the shoulder holster beneath his jacket.

Collena did the same.

Obviously alarmed, Millie's eyes widened. "It's just medicine." And she lifted the plastic amber bottle so Dylan could see for himself.

She handed the bottle to Dylan. "The doctor prescribed these for my mother years ago. They're antidepressants. And until this week, she'd been faithful about seeing the doctor and taking them. She stopped. And I'm worried about her."

So was Dylan. And he was worried about what Ruth could have done without that medication.

"How worried?" Collena asked.

But Millie looked at Dylan when she answered. "I'm afraid she might have killed Curtis Reese."

Dylan had to take a moment before he could speak. "Why would you think that?"

Millie volleyed nervous glances between Collena and him. "We're staying at the hotel, and I know that Mother had been trying to keep an eye on Curtis. Last night, when he left the hotel, she took Grandpa Hank's truck and followed him. I followed her in my car."

That meshed with the surveillance video, but what troubled Dylan was why the video hadn't managed to capture the images of Ruth leaving. But then, maybe the woman had used the hotel's side parking lot. If so, the camera angle wouldn't have recorded her.

"Did you see your mother kill Curtis Reese?" Collena asked point-blank.

Millie frantically shook her head. "No. I had to stop for gas, and I lost track of her. For all I know, she might not have followed him after that. She might not have hurt him."

"But she might have," Dylan concluded.

Millie took his arm. "That's why I'm here. I want you to help her. Talk to her, Dylan. Make her go back on those pills."

Dylan looked down at the nearly full bottle of prescription medicine. And then he looked at Collena. "I need to make a quick call." He waited until he had Collena's nod of reassurance before he stepped into the corridor and took out his cell phone.

But he didn't call Ruth, as Millie had probably expected him to do.

He called Dr. Finn McGrath, a friend in the nearby town of Fall Creek, Texas.

"Finn," he greeted when the man answered. "I don't have much time, and I need a favor."

"What can I do for you?"

"A friend of a friend is taking a drug called perenazine." Dylan used the label to spell it out. "She was using it for depression, but stopped—"

"That's not an antidepressant," Finn interrupted. "Well, not a normal antidepressant anyway. It's an antipsychotic drug and is normally used to treat delusional psychosis and severe cases of bipolar disorder."

Dylan refused to react just yet. "I know what bipolar means, but please explain the rest of that in laymen's terms."

"The patient was probably having problems distinguishing reality from fantasy."

Now, Dylan reacted. He wasn't happy to hear that, and he was concerned about what else he might learn from his next question. "Would this person be violent?"

"Possibly. That's why it's important to stay on the medication."

That tightened his stomach. "And if the person went off the medication?"

"Then, there'd be a serious problem."

And that's exactly what Dylan was afraid of.

He looked at the bottle again, so he could read out the dosage to Finn, but that's when Dylan noticed the problem. The patient's first name had been obliterated with what appeared to be a black permanent marker. Only the surname remained.

Sayers.

The surname of not just Ruth.

But also of Millie and Hank.

Of course, why would Millie bring this to him if it were hers? Dylan immediately thought of an answer. Maybe she'd done that to throw suspicion off herself. But would she really do that and put the blame on her mother? *That* he couldn't answer.

So, the question was—whose antipsychotic medication was this? Once Dylan knew that, he might also know the identity of a killer.

Chapter Thirteen

Collena read through the information on the computer screen and realized that Dylan had been right. The drug Millie had brought over to show them was indeed antipsychotic medication. It was too bad Millie had insisted on taking the bottle back with her—so she could try to convince her mother to take the pills.

Or so Millie had said.

But Collena wished she had that bottle and its contents to send to the police lab in San Antonio. That way, she and Dylan might have learned whose medication it really was. A call to the doctor hadn't produced the answer because the man was out of town for the holiday weekend.

Of course, maybe Millie was telling the truth.

And if so, they were back to square one. In other words, they had lots of suspects and no concrete evidence to arrest any of them. In fact, one of them—Jonah—was doing his best to have Dylan and her arrested for Curtis's murder.

She glanced over her shoulder and made sure Adam was okay. Her son was on the carpeted floor of the playroom with Ina. Thankfully, Ina had volunteered to help take care of Adam until things returned to normal.

Collena wondered if that would ever happen.

Adam and Collena had already played blocks and other games. In fact, Collena had gotten to spend some wonderful hours with her son without Ruth's watchful eye over them. The only "low" moment had come when Adam had noticed Collena's shoulder holster and gun. That was when Collena decided to put the weapon on the top of the armoire that housed the television. It was still within reach but out of Adam's sight.

Collena checked the security monitors for the rest of the house, something she'd been doing all day. The two P.I.s were in the kitchen having dinner. She maneuvered the camera angle to the exterior—Dylan was in the stables with the vet. One of his prize mares was sick. He'd promised her he wouldn't be long.

And then on the monitor, Collena saw a car approach the house.

She got ready to alert the P.I.s, but then she recognized that car and the driver. It was Sergeant Katelyn O'Malley, her old friend from SAPD. Katelyn had called her just an hour earlier to say she was on the way and that she was bringing homemade chili.

Katelyn was also bringing medical access codes that might help them find out whose prescription meds Millie had brought over. Even with the access codes, it was a long shot, but right now, the only shot they had since they couldn't convince the sheriff to get a search warrant to get that pill bottle.

"I'll be right back," Collena told Ina. "I want my friend to meet Adam."

Collena hurried down the hall and made it to the foyer just as the doorbell rang. She threw open the door and lowered her head against the blast of arctic air. Despite the cold, she greeted Katelyn with a smile. And with some confusion. Because the porch lights were out.

When had that happened?

The lights had been on when Katelyn drove up.

Katelyn didn't return the smile. But one brief look at her friend's face, and Collena knew something was terribly wrong.

And she soon realized what.

Someone was just to the side of the door, mere inches away from Katelyn. Collena caught a glimpse of the barrel of a handgun that'd been rigged with a silencer.

"Watch out!" Katelyn shouted.

That was the only warning Katelyn managed to give before the shadowy figure rammed the business end of a tiny six-inch stun gun against her neck.

Just like that, Katelyn collapsed into a limp heap on the porch.

And just like that, the figure stepped out and shoved the stun gun in his pocket. He grabbed Collena's hair. With a fierce jerk that shot pain through her entire body, he dragged her out of the foyer and to the porch.

The adrenaline knifed through her. A hard jolt triggered the fight-or-flight mode. Unfortunately, she couldn't do either because of the fierce grip her attacker had on her.

The moon was hidden beneath the thick night clouds and, with the porch lights out, it took Collena's eyes a moment to adjust to the dark.

Then, she saw him.

Oh, God.

It was Rodney Harmon.

Even though it'd been sixteen months since he'd attacked her and tried to kill her in the Brighton delivery room, that was a face that she'd never forget. He'd found her, and he was going to try to kill her.

If she didn't do something to stop him.

She fought her way through the initial panic and tried to figure out what she could do. She didn't have her gun with her. It was on the armoire in the playroom, and that meant she had to try to use her own strength to try to prevent this from escalating. It wouldn't be easy. Rodney was a hulk of a man.

There were hurried footsteps behind her. The P.I.s, she realized. They wouldn't be able to see well because of the darkness, and if they did spot Rodney, they wouldn't have an easy shot because they might hit her. Rodney must have realized it, too, because he calmly turned in their direction and fired.

Two shots fired from his gun rigged with a silencer.

She didn't see the bullets hit the men, but she heard them fall. Mercy. Rodney might have killed them.

Collena struggled to get away from him, but Rodney already had the upper hand. He shoved his right hand and gun over her mouth, to muffle the scream she was about to let rip from her throat.

Rodney didn't use the stun gun on her, but he did use his brute strength to maneuver her off the porch. Collena managed to ram her elbow into his stomach, but he was so heavily muscled there that the blow had little effect. It didn't even slow him down. Rodney dragged her down the porch steps and headed toward Katelyn's car, which he no doubt intended to use as an escape vehicle.

With her as his hostage.

Collena knew with absolute certainty what he intended to do once he had her away from the ranch.

"No one's coming to help you," he snarled with his mouth right against her ear. He stank of cheap whiskey and menthol cough drops.

He might be right. Maybe no one would help. With the P.I.s down, it was possible no one was monitoring the surveillance screens. And Dylan might not hear the struggle. So, she fought, trying to dig her heels into the frozen ground.

"Keep fighting me," Rodney warned, "and I'll go inside and get your kid. That should shut you up."

The threat sparked a flood of horrible memories. Memories of Adam being stolen. Memories of Rodney nearly beating her to death.

For just a moment, the images paralyzed her, much as the physical beating had done the night she'd given birth at Brighton. Collena hadn't immediately fought back that night, either. And those lost moments had nearly cost her everything.

That wouldn't happen now.

She hadn't just given birth. She wasn't weak. And she wasn't going to let this monster get anywhere near Dylan or her son. Not again.

When Rodney reached for the door handle of Katelyn's car, Collena knew it was time to put a plan into motion. She dropped her weight so that her butt practically landed on the ground. In the process, she dragged Rodney down with her. It wasn't enough force to make him fall, but it did throw him off balance a little.

It was just enough.

Collena used her fists to start battering away at him. Not one jab. But as many as she could manage.

Rodney loosened the smothering grip he had on her mouth and, for a moment, she thought he was going to try to turn the gun on her. But he didn't. Instead, he merely lowered his arm and put her in a choke hold.

He tightened his grip. Squeezing hard. And it prevented her from breathing.

She gasped for air.

Felt her throat close.

Still, Collena didn't give up. She couldn't. She was literally fighting for her life and for Dylan and Adam's lives, as well. Because if Rodney managed to kill her, then he might go after them.

She clawed at Rodney, but he was wearing a heavy coat and gloves and her fingernails weren't able to dig into his flesh. With each frantic movement, Collena used more of what precious little breath she had left.

Once she was weakened from the struggle, Rodney shoved her into the passenger side of the car. With his chest still pressed hard against her back and his arm still around her throat, he tried to position the stun gun so he could hit her with it. Collena dodged it, barely, and kicked at him.

That's when her shoulder brushed against something metal.

The keys that'd been left in the ignition.

Though she had to fight through the dizziness that was starting to overtake her, she grabbed the keys, practically ripping them from the ignition. In the same motion, she thrust them behind her.

Collena sliced the keys over his face.

He growled in pain and snapped her neck so hard she was afraid he'd broken it. Still, that didn't stop her. Collena threw the keys over his shoulder, and she heard them land on the ground somewhere amid all that remaining snow. Hopefully, they'd fallen someplace where he couldn't easily reach them. Somehow, she had to stop him from driving away with her, because he would take her to a secondary crime scene that he'd probably already prepared.

Rodney cursed her and lifted the stun gun again.

Collena caught movement out of the corner of her eye. Apparently, so did Rodney. Because he looked up to see Dylan running full speed toward the car.

Rodney lifted his gun and fired.

DYLAN DOVE to the ground just as the bullet slashed past his head.

Another half inch to the right and he would have been a dead man.

From the moment Dylan realized that something had gone wrong, he knew that it involved Rodney Harmon. That's why he'd ordered Ina to stay with Adam and sprinted to the front of the house once he realized the P.I.s weren't inside.

And his worst fears had been confirmed.

Rodney had Collena. The bastard had her. And from the looks of things, Rodney had already shot the P.I.s and incapacitated another woman on the porch. Collena's cop friend, no doubt. She was moaning and trying to move. But Dylan couldn't worry about her.

Right now, he had to save Collena.

Rodney Harmon reaimed his gun, and Dylan had no

choice but to shift his position again. He scrambled toward the porch, got behind one of the massive marble columns that fronted the house and aimed his weapon at the man.

That didn't stop Rodney. Instead of shooting at Dylan, or dodging Dylan's shot, Rodney climbed into the car, crawling over Collena. Even in the darkness, Dylan could see the struggle. Collena was fighting like a wild woman.

And then she stopped.

She just stopped.

Collena fell limp onto the seat.

Dylan shouted, though he had no idea what he said. The rage and fear came tearing through him as if he'd been blasted with a hundred bullets.

Had Rodney shot Collena?

With the winter wind howling, he wouldn't necessarily have heard the shot fired through the silencer. It would have blended in with the other sounds of the struggle.

A sickening sense of dread came with the rage and fear. Dylan wanted nothing more than to shoot at the SOB, but he couldn't, because Rodney grabbed hold of Collena and pulled her in front of him like a shield.

"Come closer, and you both die," Rodney warned.

Collena still didn't move, but Rodney had her in such a choke hold that Dylan figured he might have strangled her unconscious. At least he prayed that's what had happened. Collena couldn't be dead. And she didn't appear to be bleeding.

Still using her as cover, Rodney dragged her several feet from the car. He stooped and began to feel around the yard. He was looking for something. But what? Dylan couldn't take the chance that he might find it. And he couldn't waste any more time, either.

Collena and her cop friend needed medical attention.

Dylan watched Rodney and tried to calculate the best time to make his move. Anything he did could be dangerous for both Collena and him, but doing nothing was equally dangerous.

When Rodney looked down at the ground, Dylan knew it was time. He sprang from his position and, while trying to keep his gun ready, Dylan charged the man. Rodney looked up, cursed and tried to take another shot at Dylan.

But Dylan got to him first.

Hoping that he didn't hurt Collena any more than she already was, Dylan launched himself at Rodney, and all three of them went down to the frozen ground.

Dylan tried to move Collena out of the way, but she was totally unconscious. Her deadweight was to his advantage because Rodney was beneath her and unable to maneuver his gun so that he could shoot.

Moving fast, Dylan shifted to the side and dragged Rodney with him. Rodney outsized him by a good forty pounds, but Dylan had something that Rodney didn't—the overwhelming need to protect Collena.

Dylan drew back his fist and slammed it into the man's jaw. Rodney's head fell back, and he didn't try to put his hands up to defend himself. In the back of Dylan's mind, he realized that wasn't good.

But he realized it just a second too late.

Dylan felt the jolt. As if a million tiny needles had been shot into his body.

He tried to reach for Rodney, but he couldn't make his hands or legs move. He couldn't make anything move.

Dylan couldn't even break his fall when he landed face-first on the ground next to Collena.

The world collapsed around him.

And Dylan could only lie there as Rodney carried Collena away.

Chapter Fourteen

For Collena, everything was off kilter.

She couldn't move, and it took every ounce of her mental energy just to hold a brief thought in her head. Only one thought kept repeating—Rodney Harmon had kidnapped her.

And he'd used a stun gun on Dylan and her.

Collena forced her eyes open, but her vision was blurry. Still, she could tell that she was riding in a car. A glance over to the driver's seat, and she confirmed what she already feared.

Rodney was behind the wheel. He had apparently hotwired the car, and he was driving her to her death.

"Don't think about doing anything stupid," Rodney snarled.

She looked down to where his right hand held a gun pointed directly at her rib cage.

"You're going to kill me anyway," she managed to say, through her words were slurred. "Why should I cooperate?"

"Because I'm not going to kill you at this exact moment." He said it almost gleefully. "Well, unless you don't give me a choice. I'll kill you now if I have to."

She needed to escape.

Collena glanced around, not moving, using only her eyes. Everything was white, still covered with snow, but she recognized something. Thanks to the clouds moving from in front of the moon, she saw the remnants of an old barn. She'd been here before. She had checked out this area days earlier when she was trying to figure out the best way to get onto Dylan's property and hopefully get a look at Adam. In fact, if some live oak trees hadn't been in the way, she probably could have seen the wrought iron gates that fronted the property.

Did that mean Dylan would follow them?

Yes, of course, he would.

Once the effect of the stun gun wore off. Which could be five minutes from now, maybe more. But by then, it might be too late.

"You thought you could outsmart me," Rodney taunted. He shoved the gun even harder against her ribs, causing her to grimace in pain. "But I proved who's the smarter one, now, didn't I? I got out of jail. And then I got me a plan to come after you. The plan worked, too. Well, with a few hitches."

"You mean, Dylan," she mumbled.

"No. I figured he'd get in the way. I'd counted on him and was ready to kill him if necessary. But I hadn't counted on having to kill Curtis Reese."

Collena turned her head and stared at him. "You killed Curtis?" She saw it then, the bloodstains on the sleeve of his parka. She also saw the wild, insane look in his eyes. Judging from his strong body odor and scraggly beard, he'd probably done nothing but stalk her and commit murder since he escaped from jail.

"Had to kill him," Rodney verified. "When I went to park over in that spot next to the ranch last night, he was there. You shoulda seen him. He had all this fancy equipment to spy on you and jam your security system. I borrowed it to make sure your boyfriend wouldn't see me coming."

So, that's how he'd managed to get onto the ranch. Curtis, too, apparently. It was too late to wonder, but had Curtis planned on kidnapping Adam if the custody hearing hadn't gone his way? If so, she could thank Rodney for stopping it.

Yet another ironic twist.

"I didn't leave the ranch after I fired those shots at you," he continued. "I hid from the sheriff and lay low in one of the stables. It wasn't hard to do because there weren't many ranch hands around. When I saw that woman drive up, I knew that was my chance. She never even heard me coming when I sneaked up behind her when she was on the porch."

Katelyn would be riled about that. Hopefully, she would help Dylan come after her. Too bad Collena couldn't leave a proverbial trail of bread crumbs for them to follow.

They wouldn't have a clue where Rodney had taken her.

And that's why she had to do whatever she could to save herself. She had to accept that help might not come.

"Why did you kill Curtis?" she asked while she checked out the surroundings. The road had narrowed considerably, and Rodney had to slow down on the slick, snow-covered gravel. "Why didn't you just use the stun gun on him?"

"Things kind of got out of hand. I figured it was best not to leave any witnesses at that particular stage of the game. I wouldn't have wanted him to get loose and go blabber to you where he'd seen me. You'd have had your cop friends combing all over those woods looking for me. And I couldn't get caught. Not until I'd kept my promise to kill you."

But Rodney had left witnesses with Katelyn and Dylan. He'd probably thought she'd be dead and he would be long gone before they found her body.

"I'd read newspaper articles about the car fires with Dylan Greer's sister and girlfriend. I just copycatted what I'd read about them and decided that was the best way to get rid of Reese."

Well, he wouldn't let her off so easily. If he had his way, this would be slow and painful. It turned her stomach to think what he had in mind.

He took a turn onto a side road that was lined with thick woods on the right. She didn't recognize it, but she thought it was one of the roads that flanked the ranch. If so, then perhaps he was taking her to the outbuildings that Dylan used to house seasonal workers. Collena had noticed them when she was studying the property and trying to figure out the best way to get a look at her son. If she'd been able to find them, then Rodney no doubt had, as well. Those buildings would be exactly the kind of isolated place he'd want to use to hold her until he could kill her.

Collena tested the muscles in her hands, feet and legs. They weren't a hundred percent. But she had enough strength to do what she needed to do.

She mentally counted to three, waited, until Rodney took the next turn that would lead him to the back of the ranch. He slowed down, just enough to make the turn, and Collena knew that it was the best opportunity she'd get.

Slapping her hand against Rodney's gun so it would get it away from her rib cage, she jerked back the door handle, opening it, and dove out into the cold darkness.

She hit the ground hard, knocking the breath right out of her. Still, she forced herself to move. She *had* to move. Because there wouldn't be much time. Rodney slammed onto the brakes, and she heard his door open.

Collena got to her feet and began to run toward the thick woods blanketed by the night and the snow.

She was still weak from the stun gun, and her hands and knees stung from where she'd hit the ground. It was déjà vu. This was what she'd experienced the night she'd escaped after Adam's birth.

Behind her, she heard Rodney shout. He cursed at her, calling her vile names. And then she heard his footsteps. Followed by a shot.

He was coming for her.

Again.

THE COLD HELPED revive him.

Dylan could feel that bitter chill seep into his body. And then he heard the woman's voice.

Not Collena's.

It was her friend Katelyn. She had him by the shoulders, and she was shaking him and repeating his name. But both her voice and touch seemed miles away. The only thing that seemed real was the numbing cold.

"Rodney Harmon has Collena," she yelled. "He shot both of the P.I.s so we don't have backup. They're alive but need an ambulance. And we need to save Collena. Get up!"

That penetrated the numbness and registered in his

brain. Rodney Harmon had Collena, and he had to get her back before the man killed her.

Dylan forced himself to move from the ground. He wasn't successful on the first try, but he managed to get to a sitting position with Katelyn's help. He was exhausted. Zero energy. So, he pulled in several hard breaths, hoping that would help clear his head.

Katelyn hurried things along by practically dragging him to his feet. "I need a car so we can go after her. Rodney took mine. He used it to escape with Collena."

Dylan shook his head, cursing the damn fog in his head. "We don't know where he took her."

"Yes, we do." She showed him the screen of her cell phone. "I drove here in an unmarked squad car. It has a GPS tracking system built into it. Headquarters is sending me the coordinates of where Rodney and Collena are."

Dylan grabbed the phone and looked at the tiny back-lit screen. "He's still close to the ranch. But the car's not moving."

"No." And her voice was so strained on that one word, that Dylan knew exactly what'd happened.

Rodney had stopped so he could kill Collena.

She was fighting for her life at that exact moment.

That got Dylan running as fast as his weakened legs would carry him. He raced toward the garage and tried to figure out the best way to get to the west side of the ranch. It wasn't far through the pasture. Less than a mile. But it would be a lot longer than that if he followed the roads as Rodney had.

"Stay with Ina and Adam," he yelled to Katelyn, who was following him.

"But I want to help Collena," she protested.

"I want you here in case Rodney backtracks and tries to get into the house."

There was no way she could argue with that. Ina wouldn't be much of a defense against an escaped felon, especially since the two P.I.s were apparently out of commission.

Katelyn had probably already called the sheriff and requested an ambulance. But it would take twenty minutes or more to reach the ranch, Dylan couldn't wait for them to arrive. Every second counted.

Dylan opened the garage door, jumped into his four-wheel drive, backed out and floored the accelerator. He didn't drive toward the road but instead cut across the pasture. It was a gamble. A huge one. With the snow covering the ground, he wouldn't be able to see a hole or any potential debris that could slice through his tires. Still, it was a risk he had to take.

He pushed the vehicle hard, and he kept his focus on the fence that he could barely see in the distance. There was a shallow ditch on the other side of that fence, and if he was reading Katelyn's coordinates correctly, her car was just beyond that.

Hopefully, Collena would be, as well.

And while he was hoping, he hoped she was still alive.

He couldn't think differently. He couldn't even let the possibility of failure cross his mind. Dylan simply sped toward an encounter with Rodney. One he had to win to save Collena.

Thankfully, there was no livestock in this part of the pasture. No trees, either. Just flat land that lay between Collena and him.

He slowed a little as he approached the fence, and put

on his seat belt so the impact wouldn't throw him through the windshield. Dylan did one more calculation of the position of Katelyn's car, and adjusted his own vehicle, driving it just slightly north.

Then, Dylan aimed at the fence and rammed it with his vehicle.

The speed helped. So did the sheer size and power of the four-wheel drive. There was a fierce jolt. But he tore through the chain-link fence and came out on the other side—right on the gravel road, less than twenty feet from Katelyn's car.

Both doors of her car were wide-open. The engine was running. The low-beam lights pierced the darkness, creating an eerie, foggy effect.

But neither Collena, nor Rodney were anywhere in sight.

With his gun ready, Dylan jumped from his vehicle and, using his door as cover, he turned on his own high-beam lights. Still, he saw no sign of her on the side of the road near the ranch. Or the woods. Of course, those woods were thick, and if Rodney had taken her in there, even the high beams wouldn't help him see her.

"Collena?" he called out.

The wind was howling, and in the distance, he could hear the sirens from the sheriff's car, but Dylan also heard something else. Something human. A man's voice.

A second later, the bullet shattered Dylan's windshield.

Dylan welcomed the shots because that meant Rodney was aiming at him and not Collena.

But where was she?

The sirens drew closer, and Dylan hoped that Katelyn was navigating the sheriff in the direction of the road.

Dylan would need backup if he had to go into those woods. Besides, the sound of the sirens might flush Rodney out.

It might also make him panic.

Dylan shouted Collena's name again. Waited. With his heart pounding and his thoughts running wild, he cursed. More than anything he wanted to race out into the darkness and pound Rodney into dust. But Rodney had a better vantage point and could ambush him. If that happened, he wouldn't be able to help Collena.

"Collena?" Dylan shouted one more time.

That generated another shot aimed at him. This one ripped through the top of his vehicle and sliced right through the metal. It also helped him pinpoint Rodney's general direction.

He was in the woods.

Dylan tried to pick through the area lit by his high beams. He looked for any movement or any indication of Rodney's exact position.

And then he saw him.

Just as Rodney leaned out from behind a massive oak and fired another shot at Dylan.

Dylan got only a glimpse of him, but it was enough to let him know that Rodney didn't have Collena with him. Well, he didn't have his hands physically on her anyway. Dylan couldn't discount that she was there nearby. Maybe unconscious. That might have been why she hadn't answered him.

But he prayed for the alternative.

That Collena hadn't answered because she was hiding and hadn't wanted to give away her position.

Dylan focused his aim and his attention on the oak that Rodney was using for cover. The seconds seemed like an eternity. But still, Dylan waited. Until Rodney leaned out a second time to take another shot.

Dylan fired first.

Rodney jerked back, and howled in pain. Dylan had hit him. And hopefully stopped him.

There was some movement in the woods to Rodney's right. There, among the dark shadows of the trees, Dylan saw Collena.

She was alive.

And then he saw something else that terrified him.

Just as the sheriff's vehicle pulled onto the road, Rodney came out from cover and took aim.

At Collena.

Dylan didn't have to re-aim. He already had his gun trained on the spot where he'd last seen Rodney. And Dylan didn't hesitate. He shouted for Collena to get down, and he fired at Rodney twice.

And he watched as both shots went into the man's chest.

Chapter Fifteen

"The medics just pronounced Rodney Harmon dead," Jonah Burke announced from the doorway of the family room.

Collena didn't feel guilty. In fact, it was the news she'd wanted to hear. Yes, a man was dead, but that man had come within a hair of killing both Dylan and her. If Dylan hadn't stopped Rodney with those bullets, she would have spent the rest of her life in fear that he would come after her again.

This way, she was free.

And she could thank Dylan for that.

Of course, Dylan wasn't in a receptive mood. She could see the tension still straining the muscles in his face. Heck, she could see that tension in his every movement, even though he was trying to be gentle as he cleaned the scrapes on her hands and knees.

"What about the P.I.s?" Collena asked.

"They were both taken to the hospital. You'll get an update as soon as there's an update to give." Jonah's voice was edgy, and Collena suspected he wasn't thrilled about making another trip out to the ranch.

"Your cop friend, Katelyn O'Malley, is okay. She's with the sheriff out at the crime scene," Jonah continued, his voice gaining edginess with each spoken word. "And I'm here with you two. Lucky me."

Collena tried to suppress a wince when Dylan dabbed antiseptic on the scraped knee. She wasn't successful. And Dylan noticed. "Sorry," he mumbled.

"It's okay. It doesn't hurt much."

Dylan made a sound to indicate he didn't believe that, so Collena caught his chin and lifted it to force eye contact. "I'm *really* not hurt. These scrapes are minor. And everything will be okay."

Judging from the set of his jaw, Dylan didn't believe that, either, and Collena understood what he was going through. He was blaming himself, even though he'd done everything humanly possible to stop the kidnapping.

"Could we cut the tender moments," Jonah snarled, "and get back to business? I'm supposed to collect Collena's clothes and interview the two of you about what happened. Oh, and that's a separate interview from the one I still need to do about Curtis Reese's death. You two are just racking up the dead bodies, aren't you?"

Collena ignored the jab and pointed to the paper bag near the door. "My clothes are all in there. Everything is bagged and tagged."

She'd anticipated that the items would be needed for evidence. Besides, she hadn't wanted to wear them. They smelled of Rodney Harmon. As soon as Dylan had brought her back to the house, she'd changed into a loose blue dress so her scraped knees could be cleaned.

Jonah leaned down and glanced inside the bag. He didn't seem pleased that she had done a small part of his job for him. "And what about the interviews? Let's get them done, too."

Collena glanced at the clock on the mantel. It wasn't that late, just past ten at night, but she was beyond exhausted.

"You're leaving now, Jonah," Dylan insisted. He set the antiseptic and gauze aside on the coffee table, stood and walked to Jonah. "Any statements and interviews can wait until morning."

Jonah put his hands on his hips, and his nostrils flared. "I have to do my job."

"If you'd been doing your job, Rodney Harmon wouldn't have had the opportunity to kidnap Collena."

His nostrils flared even more. "Don't try to pin it on me. That man was on Collena's tail before she even came to the ranch. She brought him here."

Dylan didn't say a word. He glared at Jonah, and the deputy must have decided it wasn't a good time to pick a fight with Dylan.

"I'll be back bright and early in the morning," Jonah snapped. He grabbed the bag from the floor. "And you're going to give me those statements." He turned and nearly ran into Ina. He didn't offer her so much as a hello before he stormed away.

"You doing okay?" Ina asked them.

"Yes," Collena lied. "How's Adam?"

"Sound asleep. He doesn't have a clue what happened."

Good. Collena wanted to keep it that way. If she could erase the memory of Rodney Harmon from her own memory, she would.

Ina looked at Dylan. "I moved Adam's crib back into the nursery. I figured you two had enough to handle so I'll stay in there with him tonight."

He nodded. "Thank you."

"I'll also reset the security system and make sure all the doors are locked." Ina didn't linger, probably because she, too, looked exhausted. It'd been such a long, horrible night, but maybe, just maybe, they would get some peace.

Dylan went to the security monitor and checked the nursery. Collena got up from the sofa and went to his side. Ina had been right—Adam was sleeping.

"You need some rest," Dylan insisted, looping his arm around her waist. He led her in the direction of her suite.

Collena almost protested, because she didn't want to be alone tonight. Not after what'd happened. But she went anyway since Dylan probably didn't have the energy to play nursemaid for her. He'd tended her scrapes. He'd bullied Jonah into leaving and waiting on those statements. Now, he probably wanted time alone to try to come to terms with the fact that he'd killed a man.

"Rodney's dead," Dylan said. He opened her suite door and eased her just inside the room. "He can't hurt you again."

Not trusting her voice, she nodded. "Thank you for saving my life."

Something went through his eyes. Not gratitude for her thank-you. It was something dark that went bone deep. Probably something to do with this latest incident bringing back old memories of his sister's and fiancée's deaths.

He reached out and skimmed his fingers over her chin. "Try to get some sleep."

She nodded. But didn't move.

Dylan didn't move, either. Nor did he take his fingers from her chin. His touch was warm.

Comforting.

He groaned, the sound rumbling deep within his chest. "I should go," he added. "You're hurt, and you're tired."

But he didn't go.

Collena just stood there, waiting, to see where this was leading. She didn't have to wait long.

Dylan stepped closer. So close that she took in his scent. Sweat mixed with the cedars from the woods. And Dylan's own scent was there, too.

She felt the shiver of heat before his hand moved from her chin to the back of her neck. She saw matching heat in the depth of his searing green eyes.

"This is wrong," he admitted. Right before his mouth came to hers.

He kissed her gently, his lips shaping hers with soft pressure. His touch was equally gentle. A real contrast. Since she could feel his strength beneath the clever fingers that glided over her skin.

"This is wrong," he repeated. "But unless you say no, I won't stop."

With that, he kissed her again, and Collena melted against him. Dylan was probably right—this was wrong. But she wasn't going to say no. She wasn't going to stop, either. She wanted him in her bed. In her arms.

She just wanted him.

So, Collena didn't resist when he backed her into the suite and shut the door. And why should she resist? His looks alone could have seduced her. The bronze-colored hair tangled around his perfectly chiseled face. Those eyes, filled with longing and need.

Everything slowed down. Her heartbeat. Her breathing. Her thoughts. Even the emotions that'd had felt so raw and damaged just moments earlier spiraled down until they simply faded away.

Her body relaxed, and the pleasure of the kiss went through her like sips of fine, warmed whiskey.

Dylan didn't hurry things. He took his time. Kissing her. Savoring her. Building the fire inside her by small degrees until it wasn't enough. That was the problem with good, thorough kisses—ultimately they only made her want more.

Collena stepped closer to him. Pressing her body to his. She put her arms around him, to draw him closer, so that she could feel the solid muscles of his chest. That satisfied her for several moments, but then Dylan took his kisses to her neck.

He didn't stop there.

Dylan eased off his shoulder holster and dropped it onto the table. Then, he slid his hand down the side of her body, all the way from her neck to her right breast. To her waist and to her hip. That's when Collena knew it was time to do something about touching him.

She went after the buttons on his shirt.

"The scrapes on your hands," he reminded her. "I don't want you to be in pain."

"Oh, I'm not in pain." Though the scrapes and bruises were probably hurting, Collena couldn't feel them. Need and passion were apparently great at numbing the body to anything unpleasant. And right now, the only thing she could feel was the ache of pleasure.

Collena opened his shirt. Found a solid man beneath. He was everything she thought he would be. Toned, naturally tanned pecs and abs. You couldn't get that kind of body in a gym. This came from years of physical labor on the ranch.

A cowboy's body.

Her cowboy, she said to herself. And she smiled at the thought of Dylan being hers, if only for tonight.

His shirt came off. He reciprocated by unzipping her dress and easing it off her shoulders. It fell to the floor.

He skimmed his gaze down her body, and the look in his eyes let her know that he appreciated what he saw. Collena did the same to him.

And she unzipped his jeans.

She kissed him on the chest that she'd been fantasizing about, and while she was kissing, she decided to sample his stomach, as well. She felt his muscles stir beneath her tongue and lips. She also felt his erection and knew that while the foreplay was incredible, that's what she wanted from him.

Her stomach kisses obviously had an effect on Dylan. The intended effect. He made a husky sound of pleasure and sank down to her eye level. He went to his knees, gripped her waist and eased her down on the floor beside him.

The thick carpet was soft beneath her. That was the only thing her mind had time to register before he kissed her and everything went a little crazy. No more slow, soothing pace. Not this. His French kiss nearly caused her climax.

But the heat was just beginning.

With one hand, he unclasped her bra, and with the other, he removed her panties. It was an incredible sensation. Her bare breasts and sex on him.

But his jeans and boots had to go.

"Condom," he mumbled, when she tugged off his boots and pushed the jeans down his hips.

Collena groaned.

Until he produced the wrapped condom from his pocket.

Dylan had obviously come prepared, and she rewarded his preparation with the best kiss she could manage. And she rewarded herself by running her hand into his boxers.

He was hot and hard. So ready. And she was ready, too. She stripped his jeans off him and arched her back so that their midsections would meet, his erection against the wet folds of her body.

Oh, mercy.

This had to happen now.

He put on the condom and entered her slowly. It was torture. She wanted all of him, and she wanted it now. Yet, Dylan held back. And he stayed gentle.

She had the feeling that he was treating her like fine crystal because of her injuries. And it was costing him big-time. She could see the battle going on beneath those clever touches and easy strokes inside her.

He wanted to take her hard and fast.

Which was exactly what Collena wanted.

So, she lifted her hips and wrapped her legs around his lower back. He made eye contact with her. His eyebrows lifted, questioning her about how far could he go.

"As far as you want," she offered.

He understood her, and Collena nearly laughed that they were on the same wavelength, even when it came to the specifics of sex.

The next stroke inside her wasn't exactly gentle.

But it was thorough. And extremely pleasurable.

Because she was watching his face, she saw the change

in him. The savage was free, and she could feel the difference in the way he moved. The way he looked at her. The way he smelled. It was something primal. Something wild and untamed.

Something she wanted.

He plunged his left hand into her hair so that he controlled the movement of her head. He hooked his right arm beneath her thigh, lifting her so that she could take him deeper inside her. And he made sure that it was deep with each long, hard thrust inside her.

Her body reacted. Wanting more. Wanting it *now*.

Collena dug her fingers into his back, trying to force him to get closer to her, but the truth was, they couldn't get any closer.

The sweat of Dylan's body was slick now. It added to the friction already there. Wet body and against wet body. Man against woman.

His grip tightened on both her hair and thigh. He moved faster. Harder. Deeper. Until the intensity and the pleasure was overwhelming.

Collena wanted to hang on to every second of the ecstasy. She wanted it to last. And the same moment, she thought she would die if he didn't give her that final release.

Dylan didn't disappoint her.

When he could take and give no more, he thrust into her one last time. Collena felt her body surrender. Dylan lowered his head, kissed her and surrendered right along with her.

DYLAN LAY THERE, trying to level his breathing. He didn't even try to pretend he had regrets about what had just happened. The main thing he was thinking was that he had a sated body and the taste of Collena still in his mouth. He wouldn't regret it.

But he was afraid she would.

She'd been through a horrible ordeal and had nearly been killed. Having sex was probably the last thing she'd planned. Still, it had happened. There was no turning back. All that was left were the consequences.

"That wasn't good," she mumbled.

It took Dylan a moment to process what Collena had said. "Excuse me?"

"That wasn't good. It was phenomenal. And that's a problem."

Yeah. He knew exactly what she meant. Where did they go from here?

"Let's just not analyze it," Collena insisted, snuggling against him. "In fact, let's have sex again tomorrow and not analyze it then, either."

He bunched up his forehead, but he wasn't about to veto the plan. In fact, he wanted her again tonight. "So, we just…float?"

She nodded. "It's better than the alternative."

It would probably be nice for a while, especially since they had a mountain of other problems to deal with.

Still, they couldn't *float* forever.

"Will you want a divorce?" she asked.

Stunned, Dylan looked down at her. It was definitely an odd thing to ask a man while she was still naked in his arms. "What?"

"A divorce," she said as if that clarified everything. He just kept staring at her until she continued. "Because with

Curtis dead, there won't be a custody battle. At least not between him and us."

"There won't be one between us, either," he assured her. But he wasn't the only one driving that, now was he? Collena had a huge say in it, and he wondered if that's what she was trying to tell him now. "Do you want a divorce?"

Collena didn't answer.

Because the lights went out.

There was the slight beeping sound that came from the security monitor. The entire system had a backup generator so the monitor stayed on, and its milky-blue screen practically lit up the room.

Dylan got up and, in the same motion, he reached for his jeans. The monitor beeped again. It was soft. Hardly alarming. But he had a bad feeling that those two little beeps meant big trouble.

"What is it?" Collena asked. She got up, as well, and reached for her clothes.

Dylan hurried to the monitor and switched it to the main panel so he could see which alarm had been triggered. It was the back door that led from outside into the kitchen.

According to the monitor, the door was open.

He pushed the intercom button into Ina's room. "Did you leave the back door open?" he asked softly so that he wouldn't wake Adam.

"No," Ina answered immediately. Her voice was soft, too, but not so soft that Dylan didn't hear the concern in it. "And I hear footsteps in the kitchen. Dylan, I think we might have an intruder in the house."

Chapter Sixteen

"Lock the door, take Adam and go in your bathroom. Lock that door, too," Collena heard Dylan tell Ina. "And call the sheriff. Call me immediately if anyone tries to break into the room. I'll be there as soon as I've checked things out."

Collena's heart went to her knees. No, no, no! This couldn't be happening. They'd already been through so much.

"It's probably nothing," Dylan told her. He pulled on his boots and grabbed his gun. "Some of the ranch hands might have come back from the Thanksgiving break. They're probably looking for a late-night snack."

"Would they have known the code to disarm the security system?" she asked.

"One or two of them do."

She latched on to that hope. But Collena knew it could be something sinister. After all, there'd been violence in Dylan's life before she'd come into it. Violence associated with his personal relationships. It hadn't surfaced in years, but then, he hadn't been in a relationship in years, either.

Until now.

It was all over town that they were a couple. The wrong

person could have heard that information and decided it was time to kill again.

While he shoved his cell phone into his pocket, Dylan scanned through the various camera angles of the house. Collena stood by him and watched, as well, hoping she would see something to help soothe their concerns. He went through each area, including the kitchen, but because the electricity was off, it was impossible to see if anyone was hiding in the shadows.

"Wait here." Dylan reached for the doorknob, but Collena stopped him.

"You need backup in case that's not a ranch hand out there." A ranch hand would have called out to let Dylan or Ina know that he was in the house.

An intruder, or a killer, wouldn't do that.

For a moment, she thought Dylan might argue with her and insist that she wait there, but then he nodded, probably because he knew that he did indeed need backup. "Stay behind me, and don't you dare take any unnecessary risks."

Collena returned the nod. "We'll do what it takes to protect Adam."

That was all she had to say to get him moving.

The kitchen was on the other side of the house, but it was much closer to the nursery. Too close. "Does Ina have a gun?" she whispered to Dylan.

"She does. And she knows how to use it. But I don't know if she has it with her or not."

Collena prayed that she did but that the woman wouldn't have to defend Adam and herself. They had to make sure that didn't happen.

Moving quietly and staying close to the wall, they started down the pitch-black hall. Unfortunately, the corridor was open on both ends, and both ends had L-shapes that opened into other halls or rooms. That meant the intruder could come at them from either direction. Collena turned and walked backward so she could cover one end of the area and Dylan could cover the other.

Outside, the wind was battering against the row of windows that lined the corridor. Shrubs rustled. Even her own breath contributed to the sounds. It was uneven and came out in rough gusts. She could even hear the swish of the pendulum of the grandfather clock in the foyer.

What Collena couldn't hear were footsteps other than their own.

That wasn't necessarily a good sign. If the intruder knew the layout of the house—and he or she likely did—then there were many ways to ambush them without being heard.

But who would do this?

Jonah, maybe. Or Ruth, Millie or Hank? Of course, there was another possibility—a killer that had already struck twice with Dylan's fiancée and sister. A killer whose identity they didn't even know.

The moonlight bled through the bare vein-shaped limbs of the shrubs outside the windows and cast eerie shadows on the walls like a skeleton's fingers. The shadows moved and slashed with each new gust of wind.

Dylan stopped and lifted his hand so that she would stop, as well. Collena looked and listened, trying to pick through all those other shadows and sounds to see what had alarmed him.

And then she heard it.

Footsteps.

They were coming from the end of the hall that she was

facing. Dylan whirled around in that direction and aimed his gun.

But just like that, the footsteps stopped.

They stood there waiting. Collena tried to figure out the best way to neutralize this person. The simple approach might work, especially if this was some ranch hand who'd come into the house and then gotten spooked by the electrical failure.

"Call out to the person," Collena whispered.

Because Dylan's arm was touching hers, she felt his muscles stiffen. But he obviously agreed with her idea because he stepped in front of her.

Get down, he mouthed.

She did. Collena crouched and then steadied her shooting wrist with her left hand. She didn't want her aim to be off in case things turned ugly.

"Who's there?" Dylan said. It wasn't a shout, but his voice practically echoed through the corridor.

Silence.

There were no footsteps to indicate the person was running away. Nor was there any acknowledgment. So, they had their answer.

This wasn't a ranch hand.

And whoever it was waited just around the corner, less than thirty feet away. But what did this person want?

For Collena, the answer was simple: the killer wanted her because she'd gotten involved with Dylan.

But so far, the other attacks hadn't involved Dylan. So, if this was his blast-from-the-past killer, then why try to do this here at the house?

Unless the person fully intended to kill Dylan, as well.

"If you're after me," Collena called out, "then leave Dylan out of this."

That earned her a nasty glare from Dylan.

It also earned her some movement from the intruder. There was a shuffling sound. Followed by a slight bump against the wall. And someone mumbled something. Collena's comment had definitely caused a reaction.

Hopefully, it was the right reaction.

Collena saw the shadow then. The person didn't step out from cover, but she saw the hand.

And the gun.

Just as the person fired at them.

THE NIGHTMARE HAD RETURNED.

But this wasn't a dream, and the bullet that'd slammed into the wall just over their heads wasn't some uncon-firmed fear over what had happened in the past.

That bullet was real.

And it'd come damn close to hitting them.

Dylan shoved Collena to the floor, and he maneuvered himself so that he was in front of her. That way, if the in-truder shot at them again, he'd be in a better position to protect her and return fire.

Judging from Collena's muffled protest, she didn't like that idea. But Dylan wasn't giving her a choice. He'd al-ready lost two women in his life, and he wasn't about to lose another.

While he was there, crouched over Collena, he went through the other possibilities, none of them good. He might have a killer in his home. Or maybe a kidnapper who'd come for Adam. After all, he was a wealthy man, and anyone who'd heard about the recent shooting in the woods might have thought this was the perfect time to commit another crime.

But that didn't make sense.

If this was a kidnapping, why hadn't the person just gone after Adam? And why try to kill him, the person who would be paying the ransom for the child?

Part of Dylan was elated that this might not be connected to Adam. But he couldn't be that happy, because Collena's life was on the line, and they almost certainly had a killer in the house.

He saw the gloved hand jut out again. The shooter didn't aim or peer out from around the corner to determine their position before firing.

This shot smashed into the window a good ten feet away from them, and the wind howled through the now gaping hole left in the glass. But that shot told Dylan exactly what he needed to know.

That Collena could escape.

Because the shooter wasn't aiming. That would have required the person to leave cover and be exposed to gunfire.

"Crawl to the opposite end of the hall," he whispered to Collena. "And get into the family room. I'll be right behind you."

Until he'd added that last part, Collena had been shaking her head. But that stopped her, and after a few moments of hesitation, she started inching her way backward.

Dylan did, as well.

However, he kept watch to make sure the shooter didn't jump out with guns blazing. He also listened for the sound of footsteps in case this SOB decided to backtrack and sneak up behind them. Of course, that would mean the person knew the layout of the house.

Collena and he crawled back. Inch by inch. Dylan's adrenaline level was sky-high, and with each passing second, it got even higher. It didn't help that the wind was screaming now. Muffling sounds that shouldn't be muffled.

He cursed himself, for not doing more to prevent this. Collena wouldn't blame him. She wasn't the sort to do that. But he was. And it would take him a lifetime or more to get over the fact that he'd endangered her and Adam.

They made it to the end of the corridor. Just as another shot came at them. It tore off a piece of the ceiling, and the plaster came raining down on them. Dylan used the diversion to get to his feet. He dragged Collena around the corner and out of the line of fire, just in the nick of time.

The next shot splintered the wood floor where they'd been seconds earlier.

"We can double back around," Collena whispered. "That way, we can make sure Adam and Ina are okay."

Yes, and while he was at it, he could leave Collena with them. That would serve two purposes. It would get her out of the immediate path of this killer, and it would give Ina some much needed backup if this shooter got past Dylan.

He didn't intend to let that happen. But he could use the backup plan to convince Collena to stay where she stood the best chance of surviving his.

Dylan took off his boots, so that they wouldn't be heard on the hardwood and tiled floor. Collena did the same with her shoes. Once they were done, they started to move again, quickly, so they could get to the nursery.

Just in case the shooter had the same idea they did.

Dylan kept his ears and eyes open for any movement or sound.

Unfortunately, he heard one, even over the winter wind.

Someone was running down the corridor that Collena and he had just left. The shooter was coming after them, and once he or she rounded the corner, the bullets would likely start flying again.

Collena grasped their situation, as well. With Dylan right behind her, she began to run for the nearest cover—the dining room. Dylan calculated that they had just enough time to dive inside before they became targets.

But he miscalculated.

He saw the figure at the end of the hall. Just a shadow, camouflaged by other shadows that the moonlight and the shrubs had created.

And he realized it was too late for Collena and him to take cover.

The figure stepped out, a bulky, awkward movement that seemed to involve some kind of struggle. He had a split-second realization that there might be not one shooter but two. However, that realization came a little too late.

Someone fired.

And fired.

And fired.

That's when Dylan got a better look at the person who was trying to kill them.

Chapter Seventeen

Collena aimed her gun to return fire.

Only to realize she couldn't.

The person coming down the hall toward them was none other than Ina. But Ina wasn't the one who was shooting. There was someone behind her.

Someone was using Ina as a human shield.

Collena yelled for Dylan to keep down, and they tried to scramble out of the line of fire.

It wasn't easy. The bullets seemed to be flying everywhere. She wasn't even sure the shooter was aiming. Just blasting random shots through the air. Still, stray bullets could be as deadly as aimed ones.

Collena dove into the dining room and tried to drag Dylan to safety with her.

Of course, that left Collena with one terrifying question.

Where was Adam?

Oh. God.

Where was her son?

"Ina, are you okay?" Dylan shouted.

He grabbed Collena when she started to get up. He knew that she was in a panic now that she'd realized Adam might not be safe. But she had to get to her son.

Ina didn't answer right away. "I'm alive."

"And Adam?" Collena asked. She held her breath and prayed.

"Still sleeping in his crib. I'm sorry, Dylan. I couldn't get him in the bathroom in time to lock us in there like you said."

"I wouldn't hurt Adam for anything," someone added.

It was Millie.

Dylan cursed under his breath. Collena cursed, too, because she realized they had a very unstable woman on their hands. This situation could easily turn more deadly than it already was.

"You're sure Adam's all right?" Collena demanded, and she listened for any hint of a lie in Millie's response.

"He'll be okay as long as you cooperate and do as I say."

Millie's threat was chilling. And convincing. That meant Adam was okay, for now.

"Put down your gun, Millie," Dylan insisted. "And let Ina go. We need to talk."

"Yes, we do," Millie agreed. "But Ina and my gun stay put. For now anyway. Toss out your guns and step closer so I can see you. If you don't, Ina dies right here."

Millie might be bluffing, but it was a huge risk to take, especially if she was off her antipsychotic medication. Still, if Dylan and she surrendered their weapons, they'd be defenseless against Millie's gun.

"Collena's not armed," Dylan said, and he motioned for her to hand him her gun. Because she didn't have a better plan in mind, Collena cooperated.

Dylan tossed his weapon onto the corridor floor and tucked her gun in the back waist of his jeans. "I'm coming out."

"Collena, too," Millie insisted.

"No. This isn't about her."

"But it is. It's about both of you. Come out, or Ina dies."

"We need to stall her," Dylan whispered to Collena. "The sheriff will be here soon."

That might or might not be a good thing. Once Millie heard the sirens, she might just shoot them and then try to escape.

"Come out now!" Millie yelled. Her voice was so loud and shrill that Adam woke up.

From the end of the hall, Collena heard her son begin to cry and only hoped that Adam was safe in his crib. She didn't want her child getting out of the room and coming anywhere near this.

"Try to stay behind me," Dylan told Collena. Then, he raised his hands in the air and stepped out.

So did Collena, and when she went into the corridor, she came face-to-face with a woman who obviously wanted her dead. Judging from Ina's dire expression, she'd already accepted her death and was just waiting to see how all of this would play out.

"I'm in love with you, Dylan," Millie said. Her voice was trembling. Her whole body was trembling. And that meant her trigger finger was, as well.

"You don't know what love is," Dylan fired back at her.

Millie frantically shook her head. "Oh, but I do. I killed for you, Dylan. That woman you asked to marry you wasn't right for you. I thought you'd figure it out for yourself, but you didn't. Collena isn't right for you, either. She only wants you so she can keep Adam. You're too good for her."

There it was. Motive and confession. All along, the killer had been under Dylan's own roof.

"Did you kill my sister, too?" Dylan asked.

Millie nodded. She didn't seem eager to finish her confession. "She found out what I'd done. I couldn't let her go to the police. I couldn't let you know what I did because I knew you wouldn't understand. You wouldn't have forgiven me."

"No. I wouldn't have." Dylan took a step toward the two women. "You're a killer, plain and simple. That has nothing to do with love."

"Don't come closer," Millie warned.

Dylan took another step anyway and, even in the pale, shadowy moonlight, Collena saw Millie's index finger tighten on the trigger. "You don't want to hurt Ina." His voice was calm. Unlike the storm of emotion swirling around them. "You want to let her go. I can arrange help for you."

"You mean, a psychiatric hospital. I won't go. Mother's been trying to make me go to a place like that for years, and I won't. I'm not crazy. I'm only trying to protect you." Millie's eyes turned on Collena. "She's trash. Can't you see that?"

"She's not trash. She's Adam's mother. And remember, our marriage is one of convenience. For Adam's sake. There's no reason for you to feel threatened by Collena."

Collena knew he was probably just trying to negotiate, to buy some time until he could distract Millie enough to get that gun away from her. But she also knew it was true. Despite the fact they'd had sex, this was a relationship based on providing the best for their son.

Unfortunately, Millie, with her delusions and sick love for Dylan, could take that all away. And Dylan was taking a huge risk with every step he took toward her.

He didn't stop, despite Millie shaking her head and backing up. Collena's cop instincts made her want to shout for Dylan to stop. He was pressing too hard. But she also knew he didn't have a choice. They wouldn't let Ina die, and they couldn't allow Adam to be put at further risk.

Collena moved closer, as well, in case she had to help.

"Put the gun down," Dylan told her.

"No." Twin tears spilled down Millie's cheeks. "I can't. It can't end this way."

The words had hardly left her mouth when she gave Ina a fierce shove. Right at Dylan and Collena. Ina collided with them, and the impact sent the three of them crashing to the floor.

Millie didn't waste any time. While Ina, Dylan and Collena were untangling themselves from one another, Millie turned and sprinted down the corridor away from them, and headed right for…

"The nursery," Dylan said. He picked up his gun and tossed Collena hers. "We have to get to Adam before she does. Millie might try to use him to escape."

Or worse.

Collena and Dylan jumped up from the floor and raced to save their little boy.

DYLAN'S HEART WAS pounding against his ribs. He had a dozen horrible thoughts that he didn't want to have. Still, he didn't let those thoughts distract him.

Adam was in danger, and he had to get to the nursery.

Because his pulse was pounding in his ears and because of their collective footsteps on the hardwood, Dylan couldn't tell Millie's position. But he guessed that she was using the west hall to get the nursery. Collena and he were using the east.

Millie's route was slightly shorter.

But she didn't have as much at stake as Collena and he did.

Dylan turned the corner, mere feet away from the nursery door. He could hear Adam's soft sobs, as if he were trying to go back to sleep, but Millie was nowhere in sight.

However, the nursery door was wide-open.

Collena tried to bolt past him, but Dylan restrained her just in case Millie was inside the doorway, waiting to ambush them.

There was another problem, as well. The door directly across from the nursery was open, too. That was Ruth's room, and Millie could easily be hiding there. Either way, Dylan couldn't risk her firing any more shots. One way or another, he had to get that gun away from her.

He heard the sirens from the sheriff's car and knew there wasn't much time. Millie would know it, too, and she might already be in the nursery. She could even escape out the window with Adam.

Dylan hated to put Collena's life at further risk, but he didn't have a choice. He tipped his head to the nanny's room. *You go there,* he mouthed. *I'll go into the nursery.*

She swallowed hard and then nodded. Collena looked as if she wanted to say something to him, but both knew there wasn't time for that. Aiming her gun, she slipped around him and eased into the room.

Dylan went in the other direction.

Adam stopped crying. Dylan preferred the tears. It let him know that his son was okay and that he was nearby.

Without the sounds of the little boy's cries, Dylan had no idea if he was still in the nursery.

He stepped cautiously into the room. Watching his back. And trying to watch Collena's. He went to the crib. Adam was indeed there.

Thank God.

His son's eyes were closed, and he was sucking his thumb.

Dylan checked the windows next. They were all shut tight. It was harder to tell if all was well in the room because the moonlight was scarce on this side of the house. The only illumination came from the battery-backed-up night-light near the crib. There were a lot of shadows in the room, and Millie could be lurking, waiting to strike.

A soft sound put him on alert. Not a footstep. More like a swish of movement across the hall.

Where Collena was.

He didn't dare call out to her. It might give away their positions. Dylan eased his way back to the door and looked out.

What he saw caused his blood to turn to ice.

Millie was there. In the hall. Collena's back was to her. And Millie already had her weapon raised and aimed.

She was about to kill Collena.

In that flash of a moment, things became crystal clear. He was in love with Collena and desperately wanted her in his life. Not just as Adam's mother. Dylan wanted *her.* He couldn't lose her.

"Get down!" he yelled to Collena. And then he launched himself at Millie.

She fired the shot anyway.

The sound and the bullet ripped through Ruth's room,

but Dylan had no idea if it'd hit Collena. The impact of the collision with Millie threw them off balance, and they crashed into the wall.

Unfortunately, she kept control of her gun. Dylan didn't. Millie kicked his hand, sending Dylan's gun flying across the hall.

Millie fought like a wild woman. She clawed at him, bashing his head and face with her gun.

"I loved you!" Millie yelled. "You had no right to do this to me."

He managed to catch her right hand and pin it against the wall. She continued to fight, her finger still on the trigger. They weren't out of danger yet.

Collena went to him. He couldn't tell if she was hurt or not, but she grabbed Millie's left arm while Dylan wrenched the gun from her right hand.

So that Millie wouldn't hurt herself or him, Dylan dragged her back to the floor and held her down so that she couldn't move.

"Anybody here?" someone called out. It was Sheriff Hathaway. Just in time to arrest a killer.

"Back here," Dylan shouted. And then he looked over his shoulder to see if Collena had checked on Adam.

But Collena was still in the corridor leaning against the wall.

And there was blood streaming down her forehead and onto her face.

Chapter Eighteen

Collena winced when the doctor flashed the light in her eyes.

"Got a headache?" Dr. Finn McGrath asked her.

She nodded. The movement made her head hurt. So did her knees, hands and her right arm. She'd injured it somehow in that scuffle with Millie. Heck, she hurt all over, so she quit trying to identify each source of annoying pain.

Dylan sat in the corner of the examining room. He looked worried, but he was okay. So were Adam and Ina. She'd made the medics check them out at the ranch before she would get in the ambulance and come to the hospital. And Collena would gladly go through a million headaches or more if that meant everyone was safe.

"You have a mild concussion." The doctor turned off the light and stared down at her. "A cracked rib, multiple cuts and contusions, a sprained wrist and you're going to need stitches in your forehead where that bullet grazed you."

"All minor stuff," she concluded, and she sent Dylan a reassuring glance to let him know just that. It didn't appear to reassure him though. His jaw was clenched like iron, as it had been during the entire ambulance ride to the hospital and the examination.

Dr. McGrath turned and looked at Dylan. "I don't suppose it'd do any good to suggest an examination for you?"

Dylan shook his head. "I'm fine. Take care of Collena."

"Already done that. The prodding and poking is over, and all that's left is for the nurse to come in here in a minute to do some stitching and bandaging. While she's taking care of that, I'll write Collena a prescription for some nice painkillers, and leave written instructions about how to deal with that concussion. But I have to figure, if she has injuries like these, then you're probably hurting some, too."

"Just some bruises," Dylan assured him.

The doctor grunted. He paused as if waiting for Dylan to change his mind. A couple of seconds later, Dr. McGrath huffed again and headed out.

"You should be examined," Collena insisted. "Just in case."

Dylan pushed himself away from the wall and walked to her. Slowly. Almost cautiously. He eased down on the examining table beside her. "I'm so sorry."

Collena blinked and tried to brace herself for more bad news. "For what?"

"For Millie."

"Oh." *That.* She shrugged and realized she should have anticipated that he would react this way. "What Millie did wasn't your fault."

"But it was. I should have figured it out before she attacked us."

Even though it was painful, Collena managed a smirk. "You don't have ESP." She pressed her fingertips over his mouth when he started to say something else.

"Millie's in jail?" Collena asked, sliding her fingers

from his mouth to his chin. She held the touch a moment longer before she dropped her hand back into her lap.

"Yes. Hank called me on the way over. The sheriff's going to transfer Millie to a psychiatric hospital in San Antonio as soon as the paperwork is done." He paused. "Millie confessed everything."

That included the murders of Dylan's sister and fiancée. Dylan would probably still blame himself for that, as well. It would take time for him to heal. Far more time than it would for her superficial wounds.

Would he allow her to help him heal?

Perhaps not.

Collena hated to think of the future. Even though it certainly looked rosier than it had just two days ago. Curtis Reese was no longer around to try to claim custody of Adam. Rodney Harmon was dead. And Millie, the person who'd made Dylan's life hell for years, was in custody and would be locked away for the rest of her life.

Still, there were so many things left unsettled between them.

What the heck were they going to do now?

Collena made eye contact with Dylan, but he looked away. He scraped his thumbnail over her plastic hospital bracelet. "Hank told me that Millie admitted to the threatening phone call and to putting the newspaper outside your door."

"So it was her and not Rodney," Collena said under her breath. "I thought he might have been the one to make the call."

The silence returned. It was filled with tension, on her part anyway. Dylan seemed to be in a dark mood. Since the danger was over, she had to wonder if she was the reason for his state of mind.

"It'll be okay," she assured him.

Now, his eyes came to hers. Oh, they were intense. Something was obviously on his mind, and Collena thought she knew what it was. Instead of putting him through the agony of how to say what he wanted to say, she decided to get everything out there so they could hopefully deal with it.

"We can start fresh," Collena began. "Without the threat from Curtis, we can get—" She stopped when she heard a wonderful sound coming from outside the room.

It was Adam, and he was chattering.

"I had Ina drive Adam here for a short visit," Dylan explained, standing. "I thought he'd cheer you up. Are you up to seeing him?"

"I'm always up to seeing him. But I'm not the one who needs cheering up."

If he heard that last part, he didn't react to it. Dylan opened the door and motioned for Ina to come inside. She was holding Adam in her arms. But not for long. Adam immediately reached for Dylan, and he took the little boy and brought him to the examining table.

"Hi," Adam greeted. And he almost got the *"h"* sound in there.

Despite the twinge of pain it caused her, Collena grinned from ear to ear. She'd never grow tired of this precious little boy. Just seeing him made all the pain worth it.

Dylan sat next to her again so that Collena could kiss Adam's cheek. Unfortunately, Adam wasn't interested in the kiss. He was interested in the now-cleaned bullet slice on Collena's forehead. Adam frowned and tried to touch it, but Collena took her son's hand instead and kissed his fingers one by one.

Adam laughed.

"Ruth called on the way over here," Ina said, walking closer. "Hank and she are leaving town. Once they're settled, she'll give you a call, but she wanted you both to know she's real sorry for what happened. She didn't know what Millie was up to, and Ruth hopes one day you'll be able to get past all this hurt. She's gonna try to get past it, too, and start seeing a doctor again."

Collena was about to suggest that Dylan call them, especially since neither Ruth, nor Hank appeared to have been involved in Millie's criminal activities. But maybe it was best if they had some time apart.

"We'd better not stay much longer," Ina said, eyeing the wound on Collena's head. "Besides, I need to get this little one back. He's probably wanting some breakfast by now."

Collena grabbed one last kiss from Adam, and Dylan did, as well, before Ina whisked the baby away.

"Breakfast," Collena repeated. "Maybe if this wound gets stitched up in time, we'll be able to make it back to the ranch before Adam's morning nap. It'd be nice to spend some quiet time with him."

He nodded. That was it. His only reaction. Which brought her back to what they'd been discussing before Ina and Adam arrived. However, Dylan spoke before she could continue.

"A fresh start, you said before Ina got here." He paused a moment. "I think that's a good idea."

She was afraid of that, but Collena had no intention of holding him to the vows they'd made in desperation. "I can start the paperwork."

His eyebrows lifted, and he studied her. "What do you mean?"

She had to clear away the lump in her throat first. Mercy, this wasn't easy. "There's no need for you to stay married to me. We'll work out a custody arrangement with Adam."

Dylan just stared at her.

"And I was thinking about moving to Greer," Collena continued. "That way, I'll be closer to Adam."

His stare turned to a scowl. "You call that a fresh start?"

"Why, what did you have in mind?"

He looked on the verge of answering her. But he didn't say a word. Instead, Dylan leaned in, cupped her chin gently and kissed her. Even with all her aches and pains, it was potent.

"I like your plan better than mine," she let him know.

"That wasn't a plan. That was foreplay." He shrugged. "But we'll have to wait for you to mend before we carry that any further."

Collena disagreed with another kiss, one that left her breathless.

"Will you marry me?" Dylan asked with his mouth still against hers.

That left her breathless, too.

"We're already married," she pointed out.

"We entered into an arrangement for Adam's sake. I don't want that now. I want more. A lot more."

Collena felt her heart swell. "How much more?" she whispered.

"I want everything. You. Adam. A marriage. A real family. Maybe even more kids."

Now, she was breathless and speechless, and all those aches and pains seemed to melt away.

"Well?" Dylan prompted. "What's your answer?"

As if trying to convince her, he kissed her again.

But Collena didn't need convincing. "I was ready to say yes the minute you kissed me."

"Why?" he asked.

Ah, this was easy. Collena didn't even have to think about it. "Because I'm in love with you. Because you're Adam's dad. And because you're great in bed." Despite the light comment, she had to blink back tears. Happy tears, though. "What about you? Why did you ask me to marry you?"

"Because I love you."

That was it. Nothing more. And Collena realized that was the only thing she needed to hear.

Mills & Boon® Intrigue brings you
a sneak preview of…
Debra Webb's

Colby Rebuilt

Shane Allen is a man unlike any Mary Jane
Brooks has ever known. Maybe that's because
he's a Colby man – and to save her life he'll have
to become a human target!

Don't miss this thrilling new story available
next month in Mills & Boon® Intrigue.

Colby Rebuilt

by

Debra Webb

Shane Allen stared at the blinking light on the telephone for five seconds, which lapsed into ten, then twenty before he decided to pick up the receiver. He didn't want to take this call, now or ever, but he had little choice in the matter.

He pressed the blinking button and said, "Shane Allen."

"Mr. Allen, this is Harry Rosen, attorney for—"

"I know who you are," Shane interrupted. He didn't want to hear the man explain how he represented Shane's ex-wife. He also didn't want to hear how his petition for visitation rights was totally unfounded. It seemed impossible that the woman he had once loved could do this, but she had. Matt wasn't his son, but Shane had loved him for three years as if he were. It just wasn't fair that because the marriage had ended he was now supposed to stop loving the little boy and never see him again.

Nor was it fair that his former partner was the reason his life had gone to hell in such a hurry.

"Your attachment to Matthew is understandable," Rosen began. "But you have no legal recourse when it comes to Sharon's son. You surely know this."

Yeah, Shane knew. But that didn't mean he had to like it. He leaned back in his chair and forced himself to take a breath before he said something he would be sorry for later. "I suppose I was hoping Sharon would do the right thing since her son is the one who's going to be hurt by this battle." The kid's own father had already abandoned him without a backward glance. How was a five-year-old supposed to cope with losing the second person he'd trusted with his little heart?

The question infuriated Shane all the more.

"Mr. Allen, it would be in your best interest, as well as the boy's, if we moved past this issue. Sharon is relocating to Denver with her new husband, and there won't be any easy way for you to have access to Matt. Quite honestly, children of this age are rather resilient. Matt will forget all about you in a far shorter time than you realize…if you allow him to. I'm certain you have his best interests at heart. Do you really want him to feel unsettled any longer than necessary?"

Fury unfurled in Shane's gut. He wanted to reach through the phone and strangle this guy. Shane's relationship with Matt wasn't like last season's baseball statistics or an old toy to be set aside and forgotten. Didn't anyone see this besides him?

"I'll see you in court, Rosen," Shane warned. "Have a nice day." He hung up the phone and pushed to his feet. How the hell could the law allow this kind of thing to happen?

He paced the narrow expanse of floor space in front of his desk in an attempt to wear off some of the adrenaline. It didn't help. He stopped at the window and stared out at the November afternoon. Life went on even when things were damned wrong. Not that Shane still had any feelings for his ex—he didn't. Not in the least. But the kid...well that was a different story. He couldn't just pretend he didn't love the boy. Shane couldn't imagine never seeing Matt again.

A quick, short burst of sound echoed from the phone on his desk, alerting him to an internal call. Until the official hearing, there was nothing he could do. He might as well focus on work. He crossed to his desk and picked up the receiver. "Allen."

"Mr. Allen, this is Darla."

The new receptionist. She still addressed everyone at the Colby Agency as mister or missus. He'd done that, too, for the first couple of months.

"Have I missed an appointment?" He didn't remember anything on his calendar this afternoon. Still, he double-checked even as he asked the question.

"No, sir. There's a visitor in with Mrs. Colby-

Camp, and she would like you to join them in her office if you're available."

Sounded like he had a new assignment. Whenever he was called to Victoria's office, it usually involved an incoming case. He could definitely use the distraction. Working a case would keep his mind off Matt…and the hearing…and his ex.

"I'm on my way." He thanked Darla and settled the receiver back into its cradle. Taking a moment, he cleared his head of personal issues, then grabbed his notebook and headed for the boss's office.

The long stretch of corridor outside Shane's office went in both directions and was flanked by doors on both sides. At the end, near the stairwell, was Victoria's office. The layout was similar to the one in the old building, according to his colleagues. The décor was cutting-edge contemporary with a definite elegant flair. Very different from the monochromatic beige of his last workspace as a U.S. Marshal.

Shane had hired on with the Colby Agency right after New Year's. His former career had ended as abruptly as his marriage eventually had. A gunshot wound had shattered his hip, catapulting him into multiple surgeries and months of physical therapy. Despite his insistence that he could handle the physical requirements of his job, he'd been forced into retirement. Sharon had dumped him once he was out of the woods physically, and he'd spent several weeks feeling sorry for himself.

All that had changed come New Year's. He'd made one of those resolutions people never kept— only he had been determined to keep his. He was looking forward, not looking back. No wallowing in what might have been.

He gifted Mildred, Victoria's assistant, with a smile and entered the private domain of the woman who had turned the Colby Agency into one of the nation's most prestigious private investigation agencies. A woman who accepted him as he was, denim and leather included. That was another New Year's resolution he'd made: to be himself—not some spit-polished stuffed shirt like he'd pretended to be for six years. Nope. Just himself.

This was what he did now. This was his future. *This* was who he was.

"Shane," Victoria said as he strode across her office, "thank you for joining us."

As the boss made the formal introductions, he shifted his attention to the woman seated in front of Victoria's desk.

"This is Mary Jane Brooks." Victoria gestured to her guest. "Ms. Brooks, this is Shane Allen, the investigator I was telling you about."

Medium height, too thin. Mary Jane Brooks looked to be mid- to late-twenties with long red hair that spilled down her shoulders in sassy curls. Her pale, pale skin offered a stark contrast to her vibrant blue eyes.

"Mr. Allen." Mary Jane thrust out her hand as he approached the chair next to hers.

"Ms. Brooks." He closed his hand around hers, didn't miss her tremble as their palms made contact. That she drew her hand away quickly signaled that he, or men in general, made her nervous. He felt certain he wasn't what she had expected.

4 FREE

BOOKS AND A SURPRISE GIFT!

We would like to take this opportunity to thank you for reading this Mills & Boon® book by offering you the chance to take FOUR more specially selected titles from the Intrigue series absolutely FREE! We're also making this offer to introduce you to the benefits of the Mills & Boon® Book Club™—

- ★ FREE home delivery
- ★ FREE gifts and competitions
- ★ FREE monthly Newsletter
- ★ Exclusive Mills & Boon Book Club offers
- ★ Books available before they're in the shops

Accepting these FREE books and gift places you under no obligation to buy, you may cancel at any time, even after receiving your free shipment. Simply complete your details below and return the entire page to the address below. You don't even need a stamp!

YES! Please send me 4 free Intrigue books and a surprise gift. I understand that unless you hear from me, I will receive 6 superb new titles every month for just £3.15 each, postage and packing free. I am under no obligation to purchase any books and may cancel my subscription at any time. The free books and gift will be mine to keep in any case.

19ZED

Ms/Mrs/Miss/Mr ....Initials ....

BLOCK CAPITALS PLEASE

Surname ....

Address ....

....

....Postcode...............................

Send this whole page to:
UK: FREEPOST CN8I, Croydon, CR9 3WZ